William Sharp

The Mountain Lovers

William Sharp

The Mountain Lovers

ISBN/EAN: 9783337286903

Printed in Europe, USA, Canada, Australia, Japan

Cover: Foto ©Andreas Hilbeck / pixelio.de

More available books at **www.hansebooks.com**

THE MOUNTAIN LOVERS

The Mountain Lovers

BY FIONA MACLEOD

BOSTON: ROBERTS BROS., 1895
LONDON: JOHN LANE, VIGO ST

.   .   .   .

Dum juga montis aper, fluvios dum piscis amabit,
Dumque thymo pascentur apes, dum rorae cicadae;
Semper honos, nomenque tuum, laudesque manebunt.

THE MOUNTAIN LOVERS.

I.

THE wind sighed through the aisles of the hill-forest. Among the lower-set pines there was an accompanying sound as of multitudinous baffled wings. This travelling voice was upon the mountain in a myriad utterance. Round the forehead of Ben Iolair it moved as an eagle moves, sweeping in vast circles: the rhythm of its flight reiterated variously against walls of granite, gigantic boulders, and rain-scooped, tempest-worn crags and pinnacles. Lower were corries, furrows that seemed to have been raked into the breast of the hill in some olden time when the solitudes were not barren. Therein the wind slid with a hollow, flute-like call. This deepened into an organ-note of melancholy, when glens, filled with birchen undergrowth and running water, were aloud with the rumor of its passage. Upon the heights, upon the flanks, upon all the sun-swept mass of Iolair, the rushing noise of its pinions was as the prolonged suspiration of the sea. Beyond the forest of pines it swooped adown the strath, and raced up the narrow neck of the Pass of the Eagles, and leapt onward again athwart and over the slopes of Tornideon that, gigantic in swarthy gloom, stood over against Ben Iolair.

In the heart of the pine-woods it was meshed as in a net. The sighing of it through the green-gloom avenues, warm with the diffused ruddiness of the pine-bark, was as the sound of distant water falling from infrequent ledge to ledge in a mountain gorge. Intent by the fringe of the forest, or even upon the under-slopes still flooded with afternoon sunlight, one might have heard its rising and falling sough as it bore downward beneath the weight of the branches, or slipt from bole to bole and round ancient girths.

Here and there a hollow was still as deep water. Not a sigh breathed upon the mossy ground, thickly covered in parts with cones and the myriad-shed needles of the pines. Not a murmur came from the spell-bound trees. The vast boughs hung motionless in the silent air. Sometimes the upper branches stirred, but while the shadow-haunted plumes ruffled as with a passing breath it was with a slow, solemn, soundless rhythm.

In one of those sanctuaries of peace, where
the forest was thinner and everywhere luminous with the flowing gold of the setting
sun, a child danced blithely to and fro, often
clapping her hands, but without word or sound,
and with her wild-fawn eyes ceaselessly alert,
yet unquestioning and unsmiling.

In that solitary place she was doubly alone.
No eyes were there to espy her, save those of
the cushats and a thrush whose heart beat
wildly against her callow brood. She was like
the spirit of woodland loneliness: a lovely
thing of fantasy that might recreate its beauty
the next moment in a medley of sun-rays,
or as a floating golden light about the green
boles, or as a wind-flower swaying among the
tree-roots, with its own exquisite vibration of
life. So elemental was she, then and there, that
if she herself had passed into the rhythm of her
rapt dance and so merged into the cadence of
the wind among leaves'and branches, or into
the remoter murmuring of the mountain burns
and of the white cataracts even then leaping
into the sun-dazzle and seeming never to fall
though forever falling — if this change had
been wrought, as the swift change from
shadow-gloom to sun-gloom, nothing of it
would have seemed unnatural. She was as
absolutely one with nature as though she were

a dancing sunbeam, or the brief embodiment
of the joy of the wind.

As the child danced, a human mote in that
vast area of sun-splashed woodland, the light
flooded in upon her scanty and ragged dress
of brown homespun, from which her arms and
legs emerged as the white chestnut-buds from
their sheaths of amber.   Her skin was of the
hue and smoothness of crudded cream, where
not sunburnt to the brown of the wallflower.
Dark as were her heavily lashed eyes, her hair, a
mass of short curls creeping and twisting and
leaping throughout a wild and tangled wavi-
ness, was of a wonderful white-like yellow, as
of the sheen of wheat on a windy August noon
or the strange amber-gold of the harvest-moon
when rising through a sigh of mist.   She was
beautiful, but rather with the promise of beauty
than beauty itself, — as the bud of the moss-
rose is lovely but has a fairer loveliness in
fee.   Though her face was pale, its honey-
suckle-pallor was so wrought by the sun and
wind that her cheeks had the glow of sunlit
hill-water.   In every line, in every contour of
her body, in every movement, every pose, a
beautiful untutored grace displayed itself.   A
glimpse of the secret of all this winsomeness
opened at times in the eyes.   These were full
of a changing light.   The "breath" was upon

her: on her rhythmic limbs, on her flowing
hair, on her parted lips.

To and fro, flickeringly as a leaf shadow, the
small body tripped and leapt. Sometimes she
raised her arms when with tost-back head she
sprang to one side or forward: sometimes
she clapped her hands, and a smile for a moment dreamed rather than lay upon her face.
But none seeing her could have thought she
danced out of mere glee. No birdeen of
laughter slipped from the little lips: the eyes
had a steadfast intensity amid all their way-
wardness. Either the child was going through
this fantastic by-play for some ulterior reason,
or she was wrought by an ecstasy that could
be expressed only in this way. Perhaps no
one who had met a glance of those wild-
wood eyes could have doubted that she was
rapt by an unconscious fantasy of rhythm.

A stillness had grown about the heart even
of the patient mavis in the rowan beside the
winding shadow-haunted pool, a few yards
away from the spot where the child soundlessly danced. A clear call came from its
mate ever and again: neither feared any
longer this dancer in the sunset-shine. The
cushats crooned unheedingly. In a glade
above, a roe stood, gazing wonder-stricken:
but after a restless pawing of the ground she

lidded her unquiet eyes, and browsed content-
edly under the fern.

Suddenly the dancer stopped. She stood,
in that exquisite poise of arrested motion
which for a moment the wave has when it lifts
its breast against the wind. Intently she listened: with eyes dilated, and nostrils swiftly
expanding and contracting, like any wild thing
of the woodlands.

A voice, strangely harsh in its high, thin
falsetto, resounded from the upper glades.

"Oona!"

The child smiled, relaxed from her intent
attitude, and listlessly moved a step or two
forward.

"Oona! Oona! Oona!"

"It is Nial," she muttered. "I don't want
him. I am tired of helping him to look for
his soul."

The words came from her lips in smileless
earnestness. To her, evidently, so fantastical
a quest had nothing in it of surprise or strange-
ness.

The startled roe had already fled. The
merest rustle of the bracken hinted the
whither-away of its flight. Instinctively, Oona
noticed the sound, and her eyes looked beyond a distant clump of pines in time to see
a gleam of something brown leap out of and

into the tall fern, as a seabird among green running billows.

Almost simultaneously she caught a glimpse of an uncouth dwarfish figure moving slowly through the pine-glades.

Swift as a bird to its covert she slipped into the dusk of the neighboring savannah of bracken.

"Oona!"

The voice was nearer, but from its greater lift in the air the child knew that Nial had stopped, and was doubtless looking about him. She made no response. If the searcher were but ten yards away, he would not have discovered her. No fox among the root crannies, no hare crouching low in her form, could have more easily evaded detection.

"Oona!"

The voice was now further away. Clearly Nial had turned westward, and was moving through the glade beyond the pool. Once more she heard the harsh thin voice: but now it was crooning a song wherewith she was familiar, the words of which simulated the plaining of the wild-dove: —

"Oona, Oona, mo ghraidh:
Oona, Oona, mo ghraidh:
Mùirnean, Mùirnean, Mùirnean,
Oona, Oona, mo ghraidh!"

Then the silence closed in about her again. A relative silence, for she heard the hum of the brown bee drowsily fumbling to its nest under a bramble, the whirr of the stag-moth, the innumerable indeterminate rustle and hum of the woodlands in summer. The cushats crooned ever and again, hushfully nestling amid the green dusk of the boughs. A fern-owl swooped through the glades, whence already the sunset light had vanished, and after every short flight it would poise on a pine-branch and emit its resonant whirr. In the hollow where Oona lay there was still no breath of air; but overhead the wind stirred the plumes of every tree-crest, and its voice, vibrant, full of rising and falling flute-like calls, loudly surgent, haunting-sweet, was audible on all sides and beyond upon the uplands of Iolair.

The gloaming, creeping from under the bracken and down from amid the branches of the pines, had begun to fill the forest with veils of shadow. It was for this Oona had waited. Gently disparting the bracken, and, herself almost as insubstantial and soundless as a shadow, with one swift glance around her, she vanished into the darkness that involved the columnar pine-glades.

In the dim, fragrant May-gloom there

seemed nothing astir save white moths, which
flickered from bush to bush. The deer, if any
were there, were resting; the roosting black-
cock were as silent as the doves. The remoter
dusk was full of the voices of the wind, but
those distant aerial sounds were, as the wings
that fan the courts of Silence.

Shadow after shadow moved out of the twilight: soft velvety things, though intangible,
that lay drowsily upon the boughs of the pines,
or slipped after each other through the intrica-
cies of the fern.

Round the pool were many of those lovely
silent children of the dusk. Dim scores were
massed under the branches, or crept among the
willows. Some hung from the sprays of the
birches, peering into the ominous blackness of
the water underneath. Others, straight and
intent, or all tremulous and wavering, stood
among the reeds, the most sensitive of which
had still a vague breath of sound. Many of
these merged into the pool, but their ranks
never thinned. By every reed stood a shadow,
intent, inclined before a wind that blew not.
Of all that passed into the water not one
reached the star that gleamed and moved, and
seemed to lift and fall in the heart of the pool.
Not one crossed the faintly luminous semi-
circle that lay upon the surface. Each sank

down, down, till the star in the depths shone
far above. But by the upper margins of the
pool, where the pines ran steeply towards it,
one shadow sat that did not waver, did not
move, that grew darker and more dark, blackly
distinct, though all around was blurred or
fugitive.

The night advanced. The shadows moved
onward before it, or were enveloped in its
folds. Though in the forest no travelling
susurrus was audible, the wind had arisen
again upon the heights. Restless, forlorn, it
lifted its wild wings from steep to steep. Its
vibrant rise, its baffled fall, re-echoed faintly
or dully. At times there was a thin, shrewd,
infinitely remote whistling. This was the
myriad air-spray of the wind driven through
the spires of the heather.

With the second hour of the night, the moon
rose over the shoulder of Iolair. For a time a
gold dust had glittered along the edges of the
granite precipices. Then the summit of the
mountain had gleamed like a vast bronze altar
lit by hidden lamps. Suddenly, almost in a
moment, a gigantic arm swung upward an
immense globe of fire.

As the moon rose she emitted a more yellow
flame. Downward a flood of orange glory
poured upon the highest peaks, — barren, scori-

ated, lifeless, but for the lichens that thrive
upon snows and chill dews. The globe — in
which, as in the sun, could be seen a whirling
of light — rapidly diminished in size. Less
portentous, it swung through space in an added
loveliness. Serene, equable, its yellow glow
spread over mountain and forest, down every
broad strath, each grave-dark glen, down every
straggling hill-side corrie.

The coming of the moonbeams wrought a
fantastic new life in the forest. The lightward
boughs took on a proud armor. The branches
moved against the night, mailed like serpents
with moving scales of gold and silver.

When the first comers reached the pool
they fell upon it with delight. Forward they
leapt, and bathed their lovely golden bodies in
the water, which held them to itself with joy.
A score died to make a silver ripple, a hundred
perished to fill every handsbreadth of water as
with melted ore. When a water-snake darted
from the reeds, and shot across the surface,
its flight dissipated innumerable vibrations and
delicate fugitive cup-like hollows and waver-
ings, aureate or radiant with white fires. A
few fish rose from the weeds and crevices,
where they had lain like drifting leaves. When
their fins shivered above the surface there was
a momentary dazzle, as though a little flame of

moonfire had fallen and for a moment flared unquenched.

The dusk-shadows had long vanished. Those of the night, sombre, motionless, waited. One only remained: the same sitting shape, darkly distinct, that had stayed when the twilight had waned.

There had been no movement throughout the long withdrawal of the light, the stealthy recapture of the dark. But when the pool, save for the margins, was all one wave of inter-lapsing gold and silver, the shadow-shape at last raised a shaggy peaked head. For a time Nial the dwarf stared vacantly at the trans-formed water. Then a smile came into his worn, fantastic face, so wild and rude, and in a sense so savage, and yet with the unharming, guile-less, and even gentle look of most wild crea-tures when not roused by appetite or emotion.

The play of the moonbeams delighted him. When the last of them slid furtively through the shadows, and turned the reeds into spires of gold, he gazed mournfully at the gloom of the forest tarn. Nothing now moved therein except three wandering star-rays, that quiv-ered and expanded and contracted as though the central phantom-flames were alive, and were feeling tremulusly thorough this dim unknown water-world.

Once Nial rose. His small, high-shouldered, misshapen figure seemed scarcely human; the rough clothes he wore, patches of blurred and broken shadow they appeared now, might have been part of him, as the hide of a deer or the fell of any wild thing. When he moved it was with woodland alertness, with the swift grace of all sylvan creatures.

As his feet plashed among the shallows he stooped. For long he peered earnestly into the water. Then, with a sigh, he stepped back, and moved silently again to the mossy stump where he had sat since nightfall.

The late nocturnal sounds that prelude the dawn did not awake him, if asleep he were. The occasional cries of ewes upon the hills were only as remote falling waves in the sea of silence and darkness. The bleating of a restless stag ceased as abruptly as it had begun.

Just before the first trouble of the dawn these sounds multiplied. Ever and again, though at long intervals, there was the splash of a fish, hawking along the undersurface of the tarn, for the twilight-ephemeridæ. The hoarse gurgling call of the capercailzie fell through the pine glades. From invisible pastures came the first muffled, uncertain lowing of the shaggy bulls, standing beyond the still-crouching drowsy kye, whose breaths made a faint gray mist in the darkness.

The wind rose and fell. It had now a different sound, as there is a different note in the ascending and decrescent song of the lark. It was, however, still confined to the heights and the upland moors.

With the first sunflood there is something of the same chemic change in the wind as there is in the sea. An electric tremor goes through it. Its impalpable nerves thrill; its invisible pulse beats.

Long before Nial, in the deep twilight of the forest, saw that morning had come, he was aware of it from the cry of the wind, as it leaped against the sun.

He stirred, listening. The call of that bodiless voice he knew and loved so well had suddenly grown clearer. It was as though the invisible Lute-player who shepherds the clouds with his primeval music, had breathed a high resonant note. To the keen ears of Nial this was enough. He knew that the wind had moved from the south to the northwest: a thing easy to tell at once in the neighborhood of pines, but to be known of few when heard against remote heights and in the dark.

The dwarf rose and began to pace restlessly to and fro. Once or twice he stood still and

shook himself; then, with a searching but
unexpectant glance around him, resumed his
aimless wandering.

The wind reached the forest before the first
lances of the sunlight had thrust themselves
through the umbrage at its higher end. Nial
heard it lifting the still air of the pine-glooms
with its vast wings, and beating it to and fro,
sending volleys of fragrant breath from swaying tree-top to tree-top. It wandered nearer
and nearer: at first overhead, so that only the
summits of the pines swayed southward, but
soon it came leaping, and blithely laughing
through the long aisles of the forest. The
indescribable rumor of the sunflood followed.
As the old Celtic poets tell us, the noise of the
sunfire on the waves at daybreak is audible for
those who have ears to hear. So may be heard
the sudden rush and sweep of the sunbeams
when they first stream upon a wood. The
boughs, the branches, the feathery or plume-
like summits of the trees do homage at that
moment, when the Gates of Wonder open for
a few seconds on the unceasing miracle of
Creation. The leaves quiver, or curl _upward,
even though there be no breath of air. It is
then that crows, rooks, wood-doves, and, on the
heights, the hawks and eagles, lean their
breasts against the sunflood and soar far

forward and downward on wide-poised motionless wings: a long, unswerving scythe-sweep,
strange in its silent and ordered beauty, to be
seen similarly at no other time.

The sound was an exultation throughout the
forest. Soon the invisible presence dwelt everywhere. Every branch held a note of music;
every leaf was a whisper. There was not a
frond of bracken, a blade of grass, that did not
bend listeningly. The windflowers in the
mossiest hollows were tremulous.

When the sunbeams came dancing and leaping in the track of the wind the note of exultation, in deepening, became more indiscrimi-
nate. The bleating of the stags, the lowing
of the distant kye, the plaintive crying of the
ewes and lambs, the calls and songs of the
birds, the myriad indeterminate voice of mourning, blent in a universal rumor of joy.

Nial stood listening intently, now to this
sound, now to that. He knew the forest, and
the life of the forest, as no other man could
do. He, too, was a woodlander, as much as
the deer, or the shy cushat, or the very
bracken.

The birds that flew by paid no heed to him.
He was watching a young fox blinking its
yellow eyes from under a hollow mass of roots,
when a roe trotted rapidly close by him, her

hill-pool eyes alert, her long neck strained, her nostrils distended and quivering. He turned, but she did not swerve or hasten. Her fawn followed. It stopped almost opposite to Nial, looked at him curiously, lifted its delicate forelegs alternately, and sniffed with swift sensitive twitchings. He looked quietly into the great violet eyes, filled with a wonderful living amber when turned against the sun. The fawn slowly advanced till the velvety warmth of its lips nibbled playfully at the arm gently extended towards it. The dwarf stroked the smooth muzzle and the long twitching ears. Suddenly, with an elfish whisk, the fawn sprang to one side, spun with abrupt sidelong leaps round the funny two-legged creature; then, finding that its new playmate was so perplexingly staid, leapt away in a light bounding flight in pursuit of its dam, who had halted among the bracken, and had been watching curiously, but unalarmedly.

Strangely, it was with a look more of resentment than of pleasure that Nial turned and walked slowly towards the upper glades.

There was no one there to overhear his muttered words. Perhaps the wood-doves that watched him pass listened unheedingly to his angry exclamations, — half sobs, half vague outcries against the bitterness of his fate that

he, Nial the Soulless, was shunned by all
human beings, or by all save the child Oona,
and treated as though he were a wild thing of
the woods — and that even the creatures of
the hillsides and the forest-glades knew him,
while not of their own fellowship, to be no
human.

These thoughts always tortured him. His
unspeakably lonely and remote life, indeed,
was one long martyrdom. Rightly or wrongly
he, and others, had ever believed he was a
changeling, a soulless man, perhaps the offspring of demon parentage. Had he been
blessed with the mind-dark he might have gone
through his span of life as blithely as any wild-
wood creature. Two things only, besides his
human form, differentiated him from the birds
and the beasts he loved so well, though from
their world, too, an involuntary exile forever:
one, the faculty of speech; the other, the possession of a reasoning, if a restricted and
perverted, mind.

How innumerably often he had brooded over
the fantastic, and to him part-maddening, part-
terrifying, and wholly obsessive legend of his
birth!

All in the region of Iolair knew his story:
how he had been found when a little child in
the woods, and had been taken care of by

Adam Morrison, the minister: how when yet
a boy, a cripple and a trial to his foster-father,
and all who knew him, he had disappeared
with vagrant gypsies, and had not been
heard of for fifteen years, till one autumn he
was seen among the pines in the forest of
Iolair. He had been in the neighborhood for
weeks, though none knew of it. During that
ensuing winter he was fed and sheltered by
Torcall Cameron, or by Murdo the shepherd,
or by Alan Gilchrist on Tornideon, the mountain on the north side of Strath Iolair. For
the rest, he lived no man knew how, and slept
no man knew where. He was an outcast and
homeless: but if he lost much, much also he
gained. He knew the living world as few
could even approximately know it: sight,
hearing, smell, each sense was intensified in
him. He saw and heard, and was aware of
much that to others was non-existent or dubi-
ously obscure.

But the real mystery of his life, to himself
as well as to his human neighbors, who half-
disowned him, was in the reputed fact that he
was the child of the Cailliach.

A year before Mr. Adam Morrison had found
the puny wailing child close to the tarn in the
heart of the forest, a man who lived high on
Sliabh-Geal, the mountain that leaned south-

ward from the shoulder of Iolair, had fallen
under the spell of the Cailliach, the *beansìth*
or demon-woman.   No one knew much about
him.   He was a shepherd, but none had heard
whence he came or of what folk.   He asked
none to cross his *airidh*.   But the rumor was
everywhere held that Black Duncan — all the
name he was ever known by — was a changeling.   The minister was wont to disavow this,
but added that Duncan certainly lived under a
curse, though the nature or source of the male-
diction was beyond the ken of all save the un-
fortunate man himself, if indeed even he knew
of it.

One winter the Cailliach was seen of several
women.   Her tall figure, clad in a yellow robe,
as she drove her herd of deer to the waterside,
was unmistakable.   She was seen again and
again.   The following summer as Torcall
Cameron was crossing the Gual, the ridge
betwixt Iolair and Sliabh-Geal, he heard a
strange voice singing through the gloaming.
Looking about him he discerned a woman
sitting among the bracken, and milking a hind,
the while she sang a song that brought a mist
about his eyes, and made his heart throb.   By
her exceeding stature, and the yellow plaid
about her, as well as by the unknown words
that were wedded to that wild song, he knew

her to be the Cailliach. He fled, lest she should turn and ban him. A little later he saw the *beansìth* again. It was a long way off, but he recognized her: and even while he watched she turned herself into the guise of a gray deer and went leaping towards the high remote sheiling where Black Duncan lived.

That autumn Duncan was more than once heard laughing and talking in shadowy places and in the forest. On the first day of the equinox his body was found in the tarn. The face had an awful look upon it. The same afternoon Mr. Adam Morrison, going to the spot to verify what he had heard, found the miserable little waif he adopted afterwards. No sooner had he taken it in his arms, than a large gray deer sprang from a covert of bracken and leapt into the forest gloom. Despite its size and haste, its passage through the undergrowth was absolutely soundless.

The thing was unmistakable. The Cailliach had put her spell upon Black Duncan. When her hour had come upon her, she had strangled her mortal lover and thrown his body into the tarn. Then she had borne her doubly-cursed babe.

All who heard of these things averred that the child would be soulless. Mr. Morrison said no; that he would give it Christian baptism, and rear it in godly ways, and that God would have pity upon the innocent. The old people of the strath shook their heads. The minister was wise in the Scriptures and in the book-lore, but was it not well known that he knew little of and cared less for their treasured oral traditions and legends and obscure ancestral runes? Was it likely he could judge, when he barely knew who or what the Cailliach was? Had he not ever preached from his pulpit that there were no "other people" at all?

The good man was wrong. He admitted it, when, three years later, the child Nial — so called by Mr. Morrison in memory of a younger brother of his own, and because he had refused to give the foundling the pagan designation of Nicor the Soulless — was lost one summer gloaming. When, after long searching, the truant was discovered, the child was no longer the same. The shepherd who had found him said that, earlier in the evening, he had noticed a tall woman leading a child through the forest and stopping every now and again by some tree-bole, as though she listened for some one or to some thing. Later, when he was on the quest for the strayed little one, and as he approached the spot where his search was rewarded, his dog had stopped, snarling, and refused to advance. While he wondered at this,

a large gray deer sprang out of the bracken and
disappeared into the forest.   As soon as it vanished, the dog recovered from its sudden terror,
and ran forward, and was soon barking over
the body of the child.

Before this misadventure Nial had been what
Mr. Morrison himself called "a waefu' bairn."
Weak and ailing from the first, he had grown
more and more fretful; and his endless crying
and whining had been a sore trial to the good
man and to old Jean Macrae.

But after the finding of him in the forest he
was no longer the same.   He became strangely
silent.   Even when hungry or when hurt or
frightened, he made no sound.   He would sit
for hours and stare vaguely before him.   It
was with difficulty that he could be got to
speak at all, and if it had not been for the
minister's persistency he would have grown
dumb.

The questioning and yet remote look in
his eyes disconcerted all who looked therein.
Old Mary Macbean, the birth-woman, confirmed the general suspicion.   The child had
no soul, she said; she knew the signs.   The
Christian baptism and the constant prayers
and heed of the minister had preserved or
perhaps won a soul to it; but the Cailliach
had found her offspring in the woods, and had

lured the soul from the body, and had prisoned
it in some pine-tree in the depths of the forest.
Two or three years passed, and Nial grew more
and more deformed, more and more unchild-
like.   Silent, morose, he was never content
save when wandering high on the mountain-
slopes or among the pines or by Iolair Water
as it came swirling down its steep bouldered
channels from the Linn o' Mairg.   In one
thing alone he transcended all the other dwel-
lers in the strath, young or old.   He knew
every flower and plant and tree, every bird,
every creature, and the haunts of all and the
life of all, with a surety of knowledge and a
profound intimacy that at once astonished the
hill-folk and confirmed them in their belief
concerning him.

Then there came a summer when he was
hardly ever seen at Mr. Morrison's house.
He lived like an outcast, and was seldom met
save by a mountain shepherd, or by the two
highest hill-dwellers, the widow Anabal Gilchrist on Tornideon and Torcall Cameron of
Màm-Gorm on Wester Iolair.   Fitting company, it was said; for Anabal and Torcall were
not only voluntarily isolated from the folk of
the strath and held themselves strangely aloof,
but were at bitter feud the one with the other.

That autumn a band of gypsies came to the

strath. Some were brown-skinned and of foreign race; others were of northern blood and birth; a few were Celtic waifs who had the Gaelic as their familiar speech. When the people of the dust, or the children of the wind, as the Highlanders call these vagrant folk, — though commonly by the first designation, — moved away again, traceless as is their wont, they took Nial with them. The winter passed, the spring, summer came again, and with the waning of autumn there was still no sign of the changeling. Year after year went by, and the story of Nial, or Nicor the Soulless as he was often named, became vaguer and vaguer. It was nigh upon fifteen years later that he was seen once more in the strath. No one had heard of his return; no one knew of it, except perhaps Torcall Cameron and his daughter Sorcha, or Anabal Gilchrist and her son Alan; when one day, Murdo, Màm-Gorm's shepherd, came along the strath with the news that, as he strode through the forest at dawn he had descried Nial — a ragged, fantastically deformed dwarf, aged in appearance as though he were one of "the other people" who live in the heart of the hills. He had recognized him in a moment: but had not spoken with him because when he saw the creature, it was stealing furtively from pine-bole to pine-bole, and sometimes tapping and listening intently or muttering.

"And what would that be meaning?" asked every one to whom he told his tale, though there was not one who did not know the answer aforehand.

"It means that he was looking for his soul, —for the soul that the Cailliach won out of him and hid forever in a pine-tree, where neither he nor any one else would be like to find it."

"Until the tree falls by the hand of man, or by the lightning, or the wind," some one would add; but at this Murdo would only shake his head, and say that the *beansìth* had for sure chosen a tree that neither wind nor flame could easily reach, and that when, after hundreds of years, it would be dying, it would die from within, and so kill the soul that wailed and wept or lay spell-bound in misery within.

Thereafter Nial was occasionally seen. Weeks went by; summer passed, and autumn; and it was clear that he had come back to stay, though he never once drew near the house of old Mr. Morrison, or even sought out his foster-father anywhere, nor held converse with any one save at Màm-Gorm.

He might have been dead or absent, for all

the hill-folk knew, had it not been for Sorcha
Cameron, who told in the strath on the rare
Sabbaths when she came down from Iolair,
how her father gave occasional shelter and
frequent food to Nial; and for the confirming
of this by Murdo the shepherd, who said that
the dwarf for the most part slept in the woods,
but as the nights grew colder had begun to
take haven either in a cave, or in an old hut
on the hillside, or at Torcall Cameron's
sheiling.

"And I doubt if he would cross the *airidh* at
all," he added, "·were it not for that little wild-
fire of a lass, the bit girlie Oona, that Màm-
Gorm loves wi' all his heart and soul, an' better
than his bonnie Sorcha, for all he leaves her to
flit about like a spunkie owre the *fèith*. For
Nial will speak to Oona when he 'll not even
look at any one else; an' the lassie will be awa'
wi' him, an' no man kens the way o' 't or the·
whither-away o' thae twain." ·

And so that winter went, and then another
spring, until the coming of May again; and
Nial was once more one of the people of the
strath, though hardly ever seen in the valley
itself, except by the Linn o' Mairg or by the
running water, and then only .in the dusk of
the morning or in late gloamings.

II.

THE foreheads of the hills were bathed in light.   Sheer above all rose the aureoled peaks of Ben Iolair and Tornidcon.   The lyric rapture of the morning made a sound of rejoicing.   The bleating of the sheep was more rapid and less plaintive,` and when the harsh screams of the great eagle, that had its eyrie far above where the mountain-shoulders almost touch, came echoing down the slopes, they were so mellowed at last as to fall through the leagues of sunsea in sharp cadences.

Mists veiled all the slopes, and hid the strath.   The ·mountains seemed thus to be raimented in white and crowned with living gold.   On the heights these mists moved with furtive undulations, with an upward wave which ever and again lifted a great mass of vapor columnarly towards the summits.

Beneath they lay like suspended snow, or hung as palls; vast draperies of unrevealed day.

Even though the sunflood broke into these cohorts, and here seemed to suck with thirsty flaming tongues, here to plunge in golden bil-- lows among shallows of fading shadow, or here with a giant hand withdrew, rent, swept away, dissipated the ever-dissolving, ever-reforming battalions of rising mist, yet, as the morning advanced, the highland was still swathed.

Sometimes a boulder, at a vast height, would stand disclosed. The wet upon it, from granite boss and yellow lichen, shimmered as though the fairy-folk who weave the rainbows were there at work. A space below would give way to the sudden leap of the hill-wind; and with a rush the sunlight would stream forward. Pine after pine would rear a green banner, from which mist-veils would float, or rise and sway like flags of a marching army. Then the ranks would close in again. Flying col- umns would converge from right and left; the pine-banners would vanish, as though in the smoke of battle. A mighty swaying mass would sweep upward, absorb the sunbeams and splinter their gleaming lances, till boulder after boulder would be captured, and the bas- tioned heights themselves be environed in the assault.

From the narrow loch at the end of the ravine, in the Pass of the Eagles, came the clamor of wild-fowl. Now here, now there, as though a voice swam disembodied in that white sea, the double note of the cuckoo resounded. In a thick sob, the echo of the Linn o' Mairg came heavily at intervals. The muffled noise of Mairg Water crawled through the caverns of the mist.

Though the two mountain-buttresses at the head of the pass are so close that the legend of a stag having taken the intervening space at a bound is not wholly incredible, it was impossible for one hid in the mist on Maol-Gorm of Iolair to see any one or anything on Maol-Dubh of Tornideon. But through the mist, here suffused with a pale golden light, was audible on both spurs the bleating of trav-elling sheep and the barking of a dog, with, now and again, the lowing of cows.

Suddenly a voice rang out, strong, clear, and blithe, —

> " Mo rùn geal, dìleas,
> Dìleas, dìleas,
> Mo rùn geal, dìleas
> Nach till thunall l "

Upon the spring of the last word came back from Iolair a voice as blithe and more sweet, the voice of a woman, with the lilt of a bird in it and all the joy of the sunshine, —

" I go where the sheep go,
   With the sheep are my feet:
I go where the kye go,
   Their breath is so sweet:
O lover who loves me,
   Art thou half so fleet?
Where the sheep climb, the kye go,
   There shall we meet ! "

There was something so penetratingly sweet
and joyous in the song that it stirred every bird
on the hillside. The larks rose through the
mist till they swam into the sunflood; the
linties and shilfas and yellow-yites sent
thrilling notes from gorse-bush to gorse-bush
and from rowan to rowan. In the birk-shaws,
the cries of the merles sounded like shrill
flutes.

To and fro went the sweet voices. Now the
man's on Tornideon would ring blithely, now
the woman's on Iolair respond.

At last, as the cattle moved up the slopes,
with the spreading sheep in advance, the shepherding voices fell further apart. Instinct led
the kye to the sunlight, for all living things
have their joy through the eyes.

"Sorcha, Sorcha, Sorcha!" came ringing
through the mist; "Sorcha-mo-ciatach-nionag!"

"Tha, Ailean-a-ghaolach!" came back, with
a ripple of laughter, the laughter of joy.[1]

[1] "Sorcha, my bonnie lassie:" "Yes, Alan, my darling."

"Ah mo cailin geal, mo nighean donn, duit cìat mhor!"

"Duit cìat, no runach!"[1]

"The sheep and the kye don't know love, Sorcha, or they would stay here till the mists go, and then we would see each other."

"Let us cry *deasiul*, and turn thrice sun-ways."

"Ay; and meanwhile the beasts won't stand still! That evil beast of a bull, Donncha-dhu, who ought to be called Domnuill-dhu, is leading the way over the shoulder of Maol-Gorm. I must go, Sorcha-mo-ghraidh, or never a sheep will I find again, and as for the kye they'll go smelling the four winds. Sorcha, Sorcha! Can you hear?"

Hear came back in a sweet falling echo, the more remote and aerial because of the mist.

"Come down to-night after the milking, and meet me at the Linn. . . . Sorcha, I'm going to see Mr. Morrison again!"

"'T is no use, Alan. But I'll meet you at the Linn in the late gloaming."

"*Sorcha!*"

"Alan!"

[1] "Ah, my fair one, my dark-haired lass, joy be on you!" — "And joy on you, my loved-in-secret."

Infra: Domnuill-dubh instead of Donncha-dubh: *i.e.* "should be called Black Donald instead of Black Duncan." It is a play upon words: for "Black Donald" is the Highland colloquialism for Satan.

Then, fainter and fainter, *Sorcha!* . . . *Alan!* And at last no response came when Alan Gilchrist cried, with a prolonged echoing call, the name of his *ghaolaiche*, his heart's joy.

Soon thereafter the mists began to disperse.

Alan Gilchrist was at the pool, below the Linn o' Mairg, long before Sorcha Cameron came down from Màm-Gorm, the hill-farm on Iolair, by the circuitous but secluded way through the pine-glades.

For an hour or more he had lain there, dreaming. The first green breath of May was sweet upon the land; already a warmth as of midsummer was in the air. Pleasant it was to lie and dream by the running water.

When he had first reached the Mairg Water, after his fruitless journey to Inverglas, the village of Strath Iolair, he had thrown himself down among the fern, in the shadow of a boulder, overlooking the Kelpie's Pool. Angry thoughts were in his mind because of the minister's refusal to marry Sorcha and himself. It was a bitter thing, he thought, and unjust.

For that noontide, after he had driven the sheep on to the upper pastures upon Tornideon, and had got little Davie Niven, of Cla-

chan-nan-Creag, to herd the sheep for him till
moonrise, he had gone down by his home at
Ardoch-Beag, itself high on the mountain-side,
— though he was little there during the summer
pasturing on the hills, — to the strath, and so
by the road to Inverglas. As he went through
the village, there were many who looked at him
with glad eyes; for wherever he went, Alan
found a smile of welcome for him, partly
because of the beauty of his tall person and
curly yellow hair, which made the strath
women call him *Alan-aluinn*, Alan-fair-to-see,
but more perhaps of his own smile that was so
sweet out of his blue eyes, and for the grave
yet winning way of him. His rival, Duncan
Robertson, spoke of him contemptuously as
"the man for women and children;" but, as
others besides Duncan Robertson knew well,
the women's-man and the children's-man could
also be the best man's-man in the strath, when
occasion required.

This early afternoon, however, he had no
wish to speak with any, and so hurried on,
with a visit only to old Morag Niven, Davie the
herd-laddie's grandmother. The small, douce,
wizened old woman blessed him for what he
brought her, and insisted on telling his fortune
again, by the lines in his hands. Laughingly
he assured her she had told it to him so often

that he was beginning not to believe in her predictions at all.

"That may be," she exclaimed, half pettishly; "but it's this I'm telling you, Alan MacFergus, and what's more, it's not only the 'vision' of the love that's coming to you, but I've had the 'sight' on the lover too!"

The young man flushed, but answered carelessly, —

"Good for you, Mùimé; but sure 't is a risky thing to be seeing too much."

The old woman stared keenly at him for a moment, and then smiled.

"Well, and will this, then, be like what you have seen · in your dreams, if ever a great *oganach* like you dreams at all: —

"First, she is beautiful as this May day;

"Second, she is tall and graceful as a young pine, and moves like a hind upon the hills, an' no flower sways in the wind more dainty-sweet than her;

"Third, she is fair of face, with all the soft skin of her like new milk. But her hair is dark, like the woods at dusk, and fragrant as they;

"Fourth, she lives at a mountain-farm, and all her heart is in a man's keeping, and all her beauty is his to love, and she is the tallest,

and strongest, and sweetest lass in all the
strath, or in the big world beyond, and as
beautiful as Roscrana that was wife to Fingal
of old and mother of Ossian the blind bard.
Ay, good as Morna, which is the name of a
woman that is beloved by all, and fair-to-see as
Fiona, which is the name given of old to a
bonnie maid, and lovely as Alona, than whom
not woman could be lovelier;

"Fifth, and the man she loves is a poor mis-
guidit wastrel who lives on a hill opposite to
her, and I'm thinkin' his name will be Alan
too, Alan this or Alan that;

"Sixth, 't is Himself only, praise to Him,
who knows who this Morna-Fiona-Alona may
be; but in a dream I had I'm thinkin' her
name is Sorcha;

"And seventh" (*this in a relapse from Gaelic
into the Lowland tongue*), "I may be a silly auld
wife, Alan my man, but I'm na sae blind as
ta fail ta see through a split poke, for a' yer
havers and blethers!"

With a shamefaced laugh, Alan told her she
was an old witch, and was sheer doited at
that. Then, suddenly stooping, and kissing
her gray hair, he bade her good-by, and went
on his way.

But it was an ill faring. Mr. Morrison, the
tall, dark-faced minister, gray and lank as an

old fox, though a godly man, would have nothing to say to the granting of his request.

"No, no, Alan Gilchrist," he added, in parting, and in a not unkindly tone, "'t is no ill will I am bearing you, my lad. But neither I nor any true minister of God will wed you and Sorcha Cameron, because of the feud between Torcall her father and Anabal your mother, and of the ban laid by him on her, and by her on you."

"So be it, Mr. Morrison; but as for me I will be putting up with no banning from man or woman, no, not I, nor Sorcha either!".

"That is a wicked thing for you to say. But Sorcha is a good lass if you're not a good lad; and . . . and . . . the long and short of it is I can't and won't wed you and her . . . no, not though your mother and Sorcha's father were to die; and that I avow here solemnly, to the stones be it said."

And so it was that the young man went away wrathful and indignant. Yet, with every mile of his homeward journey he cared less and less. After all, what did it matter to him or Sorcha? Living remote upon the solitary hills, and rarely seeing the people of the strath, what did it avail whether or no he and she were " blessed " by Mr. Morrison? Well, he had done what he could.

He knew, of course, of the heavy weight of a parental ban; how, with some, it was a command as sacred and inviolable as those of God. But he did not know all that Mr. Morrison knew, or surmised; wherein, indeed, was the deeper reason of the refusal.

"The child Oona, the child Oona," muttered the minister as he returned to his house, "why was she sent by Anabal, as soon as might be after birth, to Torcall Cameron? And why was he stricken blind, he there alone on Màm-Gorm, with Marsail his wife long dead, and only his daughter Sorcha, sweet lass, beside him; stricken of God, blind and desolate for all his days thereafter? Alas, too, what of the doom of Fergus her husband!"

But, lying by the running water of Mairg, Alan, at last oblivious of what had angered him and left in his mind a vague distress, pondered other and dearer things than these.

His heart was full of Sorcha. Already, as indeed for more than a month past, there was upon him that trance of love of which the old Celtic poets speak. Even now he went daily in a dream. Malveen, the widow-mother of Davie the herd-laddie, saw him often as he passed to and fro upon the hillside, as one in a vision, rapt, with shining eyes. At times, too, unknown of either, she caught a glimpse

of Alan and Sorcha as they kept tryst in the
gloamings. She mothered them with the
longing woman's joy in love that had never
been hers; they were her dear ones, though
rare it was that she had word of either. The
youth of youths, the maid of maids: to her at
last something more than real and familiar,
remote as they were in the glamour that was
about them as the Mountain Lovers.

It was in the late gloaming, as she had
. promised, that Sorcha stole soundlessly from
the forest, and was in Alan's arms almost
before he knew that the tryst was kept.

III.

VOLUMES of gray-black cloud swept up the
flanks of Iolair. The breath of the southwest
wind fell moist upon the land. All the wonderful color of the highland seemed absorbed,
as though a sponge had been passed over it.
The after-gloom was enhanced by the silence
which prevailed, for the thunderous weight
in the air hushed the birds. Even the cor-
bies sat sullenly on stone dyke or solitary
quicken.

Up at the farm of Màm-Gorm the cloud-
skirts went trailing by, sometimes enveloping
the whole *airidh* in dark clinging obscurity,
and ever and again lifting high above it as
though with a spasmodic leap.

A few yards from the door of the low white-
washed house Torcall Cameron stood, his gaunt
figure, with its mass of tangled iron-gray hair,
thrown into strong relief. Though he grasped
a heavy oaken staff, his head was uncovered.
From this, Nial inferred that "Màm-Gorm"
was not going far: of which he was glad, for

there was no one in the house, wild weather was nigh, and it was not a time for a blind man to wander among the hills, with the sheep-paths damp and slippery, and often obliterated in the moist peat.

For, though Màm-Gorm thought he was alone, Nial had been his silent companion for an hour past. Sorcha, he knew, was up at the high sheiling on Iolair, with the cows; Oona, he imagined, was either wandering after the sheep with Murdo, the shepherd, or was in the forest with Nial, or might be flitting here and there on the slopes like the wild fawn she was. As for Nial, Torcall Cameron rarely gave him a thought. The dwarf was like a faithful collie, to be fed and given a kindly clap now and then, while his gratitude and devotion were taken for granted.

This rough, stern, blind and stricken giant was a divine being to the poor child of the woods. In a vague way, Nial thought of Màm-Gorm as God; like Màm-Gorm, God could provide, could at rare times be tender and pitiful, could be stern, morose, forbidding, terrible in wrath, of a swift avenging spirit, could strike, bruise, drive forth, kill.

When Sorcha had left at sunrise she knew that her father had the gloom upon him. In vain she looked here and there for Oona. The

child had vanished. The platter in which
she had her porridge was found under a bench
near the rowan at the side of the house, where,
indeed, Sorcha had looked for it, as she knew
Oona's frequent way of carrying her food out
of doors, and eating it in a hollow below a
rock, or under a tree, or even beneath the
bench, like a little wild thing.

She had turned, after she had called Fionn
and Donn, the dogs, and gone back to the
house, and kissed her father. His blind eyes
were upon her, though it was not through them
that he knew she was troubled. He felt the
sweet breath of her upon his brow. It was like
the first day of spring when she kissed him,
but he did not smile. Before she went away
with the cows she found Nial, and bade him
keep watch and ward, though without letting
himself be seen.

But all morning and noon Torcall Cameron
had sat brooding by the peats. At the turn
of the day he rose, ate some of the bread and
cold porridge which, with a jug of milk, Sorcha
had set on the table beside him; then resumed
his listless attitude by the fire, into the heart
of which he stared with his blank unwavering
eyes.

Nial had grown tired, as a collie will tire if
the kye drowse, chewing the cud.

He had wandered far from the *airidh*, and passed idly through the pines. No more of him might have been seen that day had he not heard Oona singing in the woods. It was in vain that he tried to come upon her. Either she had caught sight of him and wilfully evaded his quest of her, or she was like a birdeen lured by the dancing sun-rays. At the last, he thought of a song she was wont to sing. Across the midst of the high glade where he was, lay the bole of a half-fallen pine. Along this he clambered, till he reached the end boughs, and so out upon a feathery branch which swayed up and down with his weight, as a fir-spray when a cushat alights on it.

> " Wild fawn, wild fawn,
> Hast seen the Green Lady?
> The merles are singing,
> The ferns are springing,
> The little leaves whisper from dusk to dawn —
> *Green Lady! Green Lady!*
> The little leaves whisper from dusk to dawn —
> Wild fawn, wild fawn!"

It was a harsh and wild music, that song of Oona on the lips of Nial. Brokenly, too, it came, between gasps of breath, for as the branch swayed so the dwarf's excitement grew, and he seized the pine-needles as though they were the mane of a horse, and he were riding from death for life: —

> " Wild fawn, wild fawn,
> Hast seen the Green Lady?
> The bird in the nest
> And the child at the breast,
> They open wide eyes as she comes down the dawn, —
> The bonnie Green Lady;
> Bird and child make a whisper of music at dawn, —
> Wild fawn, wild fawn ! "

Suddenly he ceased his fierce ride of the branches. Surely that clear call was from the throat of Oona? Yes, near she was, though invisible. Her song bubbled from her as sunlit water down a brae : —

> " Wild fawn, wild fawn,
> Dost thou flee the Green Lady?
> Her wild-flowers will race thee,
> Her sunbeams will chase thee,
> Her laughter is singing aloud in the dawn, —
> O, the Green Lady,
> With yellow flowers strewing the ways of the dawn,
> Wild fawn, wild fawn ! "

Even the hawk-keen eye of Nial failed to discover Oona. Her voice came from a covert of bracken, amid which rose craggy, mossed boulders; and, doubtless, behind one of these the girl sheltered.

"Oona!"

He lay still now, save for the quivering of his eagerness. The branch was bent by his weight, but did not sway.

"Oona!"

The rapid skiff-skiff of a hind leaping through the fern, through the green-glooms to his right, caught his attention; otherwise he must have seen the bending of the bracken in the hollow beyond him, and have heard the faint rustle as a little cat-like figure swung herself up into a low-branched rowan.

"Oona! Oona!"

Again he sang in his strange, half-screaming, falsetto voice, first one, then another of the snatches of Gaelic song which he had learned from Oona, but without response. One of his sudden fits of anger seized him, and he bit savagely at the supporting branch. Then, with a peal of mirthless laughter, he began to sway wildly to and fro again, so that it was a wonder the bough did not break. He was swung this way and that, as an apple on an outspread branch. With short, incoherent cries he rode onwards through the air, for the moment persuaded by his fantasy that he was one of those wind-demons of whom he had heard Murdo, the shepherd, speak,— pale elves of the air who race across forest and moor on flying leaves and broken branches, or are swept screaming in the wake of the wind, as, with out-blown mane and fierce snorting and neighing, "the gray stallion" speeds with mile-long leaps.

4

A frenzy of insensate wrath shook him so that he nearly lost his grip. Screaming, he hurled towards Oona the curses that seemed to him most dreadful and mysterious, dark anathemas of old-time learned here and there during his far-wanderings.

"Droch cheann ort, Oona! Droch bhàs ort! Och, ochan, bas dunach ort! Gu ma h-olc dhuit!—Gu ma h-olc dhuit!"[1]

A faint, shuddering cry came from somewhere close at hand. In a moment his madness went from him. The dumb animal soul felt the finger of God touch it; all wrath ceased, and a great pity came, and longing, and sorrow. The tears sprang to his eyes, and he lay on the branch sobbing convulsively, so that he was like to fall.

He raised his head at last, and looked eagerly about him.

"Oona!"

Still there was no response. His gaze glanced hither and thither like a swallow. If a bee crawled from a fox-glove bell, he noted it; if a spider swung on a glistening thread, he saw her as, spinning, she sank. If a wood-lark stirred, he saw the shadow of its wing

---

[1] "Bad end to you! Bad death to you! Ay, and may a death of woe be on you! Evil to you, evil to you!"

flit from frond to frond. But of Oona, no
trace.

"Oona, my fairy! Oona, my fawn! I didn't
mean it! I didn't mean it! The words were
in my throat. I couldn't help it! Not a
word was true. Oh, my grief, my grief! *Oona
mùirnean, Oona mo mùirnean,—Ochone, ochone,
thràisg mo chridhe*—darling, darling, oh, 't is.
my heart that is parched!"

But the child was obdurate. She made no
sign. Nial lay moaning on the branch. The
silence was unbroken, save by the sea-like
whisper of the wind among the leaves.

Suddenly a cushat crooned. Then the low
croodling sound palpitated upon the warm
sunlit air that flooded in among the pine-
boughs.

The dwarf listened. The gloom in his eyes
lifted. He knew how Oona loved his one
utterance that was his own, which he had
made in imitation of the crooning of a dove.
Raising his head, he half mumbled, half
sang, —

> "Oona, Oona, mo ghràidh,
> Oona, Oona, mo ghràidh,
> Mùirnean, mùirnean, mùirnean,
> Oona, Oona, mo ghràidh!"

Surely she would respond; ah, yes, that
shrill mocking laugh, elfin-sweet in his ears!

His gaze leapt along the track of the sound,
and then at last he espied her, crouching low
in the fork of a rowan with her bare legs
hidden by the bole, and only the sparkle of
her eyes glinting from behind the screen of
leaves.

"Ah," he cried joyously, "I see you, Oona,
my dove! Ah, my little white dove, your
little black dove sees you!"

Oona drew herself up, leapt to a lower
branch, and sprang to the ground.

"*Cha'n ann de mo chuideachd thù, cha'n ann
de mo chuideachd thù ars an colman,*" she cried
mockingly; "you are not of my flock, not of
my flock, said the dove!"[1]

And with that she spread out her yellow
hair with her hands, and went dancing and
leaping through the bracken. Onward she
flickered like a sunbeam, till she came to a
rocky declivity, where she stopped abruptly,
and stared intently into the hollow beyond
her.

Turning, she looked to see if Nial were
watching her, and when she saw that he was
still on the swaying pine-branch she cried
eagerly, —

[1] A pretty and common onomatopœic saying, which I remember first hearing as a lullaby when I was a child of three
or four.

"Look, Nial! Look!"

"What is it?" he cried, nearly toppling from the bough in his eagerness. "What is it, Oona? What is it?"

"It must be your soul, Nial! It's black and wriggling about, in case you catch it! *Bi ealamh! Bi ealamh!* Be quick, be quick!"

Then, with a spring, she leapt out of sight. Nial stared after her for a moment, caught his breath spasmodically, crawled swiftly back to the tree, half clambered, half fell to the ground, and then ran like a leaping goat towards the place where Oona had disappeared.

When he reached the ridge of rock which overhung the hollow he stopped, trembling like a reed in a wind-eddy. At last! At last! Was he to find his soul at last? Black or white, fair to see or uncouth as himself, what did it matter, if only his long quest were now to be rewarded?

Shaking as in an ague, he crawled forward on his belly, till his shaggy head projected over the ledge. At first he could not see, for the passion in his heart had filmed his eyes.

Then at last he stared down into the greenness. He could see nothing. Not a wild bee fumbled among the moss, not an ant crawled along a spray of grass.

What did it mean?

Was it possible that Oona could see what he could not? Here, perhaps, was his tragic sorrow: that his soul might often be nigh, but was invisible to him.

With a hoarse exclamation, half scream, half call, he cried to Oona to come to him. He had a name for her which he had adopted from Murdo, the shepherd, and by this he called her now.

"Bonnie-wee-lass, bonnie-wee-lass, come to me! *Oona mùirnean, Oona-mo-ghràidh*, come to your poor Nial! Oh, my soul, my soul, it will be lost. Oona, it will be lost! Quick, quick, bonnie-wee-lass!"

But no answer came. There was no sign of the girl. She might be hiding near, or be already far away, perhaps croodlin' back to the doves in the middle of the forest, or chasing dragon-flies by the tarn, or out upon the hill-side flitting from rock to rock like a butterfly, or singing and springing from gale-tuft to heather-tussock as a green lintie in the sunlight. "O lassie, lassie, where is my soul, where is my soul?" he cried despairingly.

Suddenly his own curses came back to him, terrible on Oona's unwitting lips.

"*Gu ma h-olc dhuit, Nial! Gu ma h-olc dhuit!* A bad end to you too, Nial-without-a-

soul, and I'll be telling my father, I will, that
you laid your curse on me; ay, and I will also
be telling Sorcha too, and Murdo, and Alan,
and the dogs; and I'll whisper it to the wind,
so that it'll tell the Green Lady of the Hills;
and if I meet your soul I'll tell it, so that it
may be ashamed of you, and go and drown
itself in a peat-hole!"

Nial listened, quivering. His eyes strained
as a crouching hound's.

At last he spoke, —

"I was mad, Oona. Forgive me.' I see your
voice coming from behind that rock. Will
you not return and show me my soul?"

"Look in the hollow of the stone beneath you,
silly Nial!" came the child's voice mockingly.

Nial stared; then, descrying nothing, leapt
into the hollow. The next moment he recoiled, with a look of horror.

An adder lay in a little ferny crevice at the
base of the rock. Its writhing black body was
trying to get out of sight, but could not. An
adder was the one thing in nature that the outcast could not bear to look at. It gave him a
horror that at times moved him to frenzy, at
times made him flee as a man accursed.

Now, he stood as one fascinated. If the
nàthair had wriggled towards him he would
have stood motionless.

With a heavy swaying motion of his head he muttered, —

"Anam nathrach
Anam nathrach!"[1]

But when the adder saw a crevice elsewhere, that promised better, and swiftly wriggled to it, Nial saw that it was only a crawling beast, this and nothing more.

With a dart like a hawk he seized it by the tail, swung it round his head while he shouted "*Droch spadadh ort! Droch spadadh ort!* Bad death to you! Bad death to you!" and flung it against the face of the rock, so that when it fell across a bracken it lay as though stunned or dead.

A shout of elfish laughter came from Oona, who had sprung from her covert, and watched Nial's discomfiture with malicious glee. He turned slowly. His corrugated brows were knitted grotesquely, as with dull, bewildered eyes he stared in the direction of the laughter. With a furtive motion he kept shifting his weight now to one foot, now to another, occasionally dragging one backward as though pawing the ground. His tormentor knew well these signs of perplexity, and her light tan-

[1] " Serpent-soul, serpent-soul ! "
Pronounce àn' ŭm nàa-rach. *Nathrach* is the genitive of *Nathair* (pronounced *nha*'er, or a'*er* nasally).

talizing glee rippled afresh across the glade.
She stood knee-deep in bracken, with her right
hand clasping the black and silver bough of
a birk; a golden-green hue upon her from
beneath from the sunlit fern; upon her from
above a flood of yellow sunshine, so that she
stood out like a human flower, a new daffodil
of the woods.

The wild, rude, misshapen creature who
fronted her seemed less human now than his
wont, with that bovine stare, that uncouth
guise, his over-large and heavy head slowly
swaying, his restless stamping and scraping.
Suddenly it dawned upon him that Oona had
not been in earnest; that she had played with,
and now mocked him. His eyes grew red, as
those of wild swine do of a sudden, or as those
of an angry badger. A spray of froth blew
from his hanging lip. His long, horny fingers
opened and closed like sheathing and unsheath-
ing claws.

The next moment there stirred in his brain
the thought that perhaps, after all, Oona was
mocking him because he had lost, perhaps
even because he, he himself, had destroyed his
long-sought and moment-agone found soul.

With a cry he threw himself on the ground,
sobbing convulsively. He lay there like a
stricken beast, a quivering, ungainly heap. It

was no unknowing beast, though, that moaned, over and over, "My soul! My soul! My soul!" Great tears like a stag's ran down his furrowed cheeks. Oona stood amazed. Here was no frenzy of blind rage such as she had seen at times in her companion, but passionate grief — sobs, tears.

The child shivered. God surely has the tendrils of a child's heart close-clinging to His own. Perhaps the wind murmured to her, "My Grief! My Grief!" Perhaps the leaves whispered, "Sorrow, O Sorrow!" Perhaps the blind earth breathed, "My Gloom! My Gloom!" Perhaps the laughing sunlight sighed, or the wild bees crooned, or the doves moaned, "Peace! Peace! Peace!"

Oona's eyes grew dim. A trembling was upon her, like that of a bird in the hollow of the hand. Like a bird, too, was her heart; sure, the flutter of it was an eddy of joy in heaven.

She came towards Nial with swift, noiseless step. He did not hear her approach, or if his wild-wood ear caught a rustle, he did not look up. The first he knew of her was the stealing of a small arm round his neck; then the pressure of a warm body against his side; then a wisp of fragrant yellow hair tangled with his coarse shaggy fell, a soft cheek laid against his, a hand like a little white hovering bird caressed

his face. Sweetest of all, the whisper that
stole into his dark brain as moonlight: "Nial,
darling Nial!"

His sobs ceased. Only his breath came
quick and hard. His whole body panted,
quivered still.

"Forgive me, Nial! dear, good Nial! I did
not mean to hurt you so. I was angry because
of your words. But I — I — did n't really mean
that *that* was your soul. Nial, Nial, I did n't
see your soul at all!"

Slowly he lifted his wet, inflamed face; his
eyes agleam through the tangled locks that
fell over his brows.

"Have you *ever* seen it, Oona?"

He could just hear the whispered *no*. A
deep sigh passed her ears, and she pressed
closer to his sorrow.

"Oona, my fawn, do you think you'll ever
see it? Do you think I'll find it some day?"

"Oh, yes, Nial! Yes, yes, yes!"   .

"And you will help your poor ugly Nial to —
to — find it?"

"Sure it is helping you I will be, with all
my heart, *Nial-a-ghràidh.*"

He stooped his head over hers, lightly shoved
her back, and kissed her sunshine-hair. She
raised an arm, and pulled his face to hers, and
kissed him gently.

A faint smile, a glimmer of sunlight on a wet, dishevelled road, came over his face.

Oona sat back, relieved, but with questioning eyes.

"Are you *sure* you have no soul, Nial? Not even a small dark one, that will grow some day, and be beautiful, just as *you* will, when — when — you die?"

"I am sure, birdeen. Ask Màm-Gorm, ask Sorcha, or Alan, or Murdo, or any of the people down yonder; they know. And *I* know, when I look in the tarn, or in the pool below the Linn o' Mairg, or in smooth water anywhere; ay, and when the deer come to me, or the sheep do not stir out of my way, or the kye come close and breathe on me kindly. No bee will sting me, and the dragon-flies, that even *you* can't catch, rest sometimes, as the moths do, on my head or arm."

Oona kneeled, and bade the dwarf do likewise. Then she told him that his evil might be because of a *rosad* upon him, the spell of the Cailliach; and that she knew a *sian* might ease him. With closed eyes and clasped hands she repeated slowly, —

"An ainm an Athar, a Mhic,
'S an Spioraid Naoimh!
Paidir a h'aon,
Paidir a dha,

Paidir a tri,
Paidir a ceithir,
Paidir a coig,
Paidir a sea,
Paidir a seachd ;
'S neart nan seachd padirean a' sgaoileadh do
  Gholair air na clachan glas ud thall !

"In the name of the Father,
The Son,
And the Holy Ghost :
By one prayer,
By two prayers,
By three prayers,
By four prayers,
By five prayers,
By six prayers,
By seven prayers ;
And may the strength of the seven prayers
Cast out the ill that is in you
Upon the gray stones over there !"[1]

Long and earnestly she watched to see if the incantation would effect the miracle. Nial trembled, with downcast eyes.

"Perhaps there is no evil in you, Nial," she whispered; "so now I will pray to Himself for you, and you repeat what I say, and shut your eyes and clasp your hands just as I do."

The soulless man and the child knelt side by side among the fern. The light lay all about them as a benediction. The rising

[1] *Paidir* is literally a *Pater; i. e.,* a *Paternoster,* "Our Father."

wind, with a wet sough in it, came along the
pines like an intoning anthem. Around them
the bee hummed unwitting; in a tree beyond
them a cushat crooned and crooned.

Oona's voice came low and sweet as the
hidden dove's:—

> *O Father,*
> *That is the Father of the father of Sorcha and me,*
> *I pray that you will give Nial a soul.*

Silence. Then a hoarse, sobbing voice, —

> "I pray that you will give Nial a soul!"

Then Oona again; and, again, Nial, —

> *I pray that Nial may find his soul soon !*
> "I pray that Nial may find his soul soon!"

> *I pray that it will be a good soul !*
> "I pray that it will be a good soul!"

> *I pray that it may have yellow hair and blue eyes!*
> "I pray that it may have yellow hair and blue eyes!"

> *I pray that father and Sorcha and Alan and Murdo,*
> *And that Donn and Fionn, the collies, and the kye*
> *And the sheep, and — and — everything —*
> *Will love Nial !*
> "That everything will love Nial!"

> *And that Nial will go to Heaven too!*
> "And that Nial will go to Heaven too!"

> *And this is the prayer of Oona,*
> *The daughter of Torcall Cameron,*
> *Who lives at Màm-Gorm on Iolair,*
> *An ainm an Athar, a Mhic, 's an Spioraid Naoimh!*
> "An ainm an Athar, a Mhic, 's an Spioraid Naoimh!"

Oona opened her eyes, looked earnestly at Nial, leaned forward, and kissed him.

"Now, Nial, rise, and turn sun-ways, and cry *Deasìul.*"

The dwarf did as she bade; then, with a happy laugh, she slipped her hand in his.

"Let us go back now. The rain is coming."

And so, as the glooms of storm came rapidly over the mountain, the two moved, silent and happy, through the sighing glades of the forest.

Lowering skies, with the floating odor of coming rain, already dulled the hill-land. A raven, flying athwart Iolair, looked larger than its wont. Its occasional croak fell heavily, as though from ledge to ledge of weighty air. The wood-doves, which flew back towards the forest, winged their way at a lower level than usual, the clamor of their pinions beating the atmosphere as with oars; on the moorland the lapwings rose and fell incessantly, · with wailing cries. The scattered kye lowed uneasily, or stood below solitary rowans or wild-guins, easing their fly-tormented flanks with their swishing tails. On the farther slopes, the querulous lambs bleated; everywhere the incessant calling of the ewes made a mournful rumor. The wind moved with a heavy lift, here rising, here falling, anon whirling upon itself, so that all the fern and undergrowth in the corries bent one way, or, for a league, the spires of the heather whitened.

High and low, the innumerous hum of insects vibrated on the air. Thus may the hum of the wheeling world be heard of Keithoir, who dreams in the hollow of a green hill unknown of man; or of the ancient goddess Orchil, who, blind and dumb, works in silence at the heart of Earth at her loom Change, with the thridding shuttles Life and Death; or of Manannan, who sleeps under the green wave, hearing only the sigh of the past, the moan of the passing, the rune of what is to come.

Before Oona and Nial drew close to the hill-farm, a shrill sustained cry, not unlike that of the bird called the oyster-catcher, came along the slopes. Oona knew at once it was Sorcha's summons for her to help with the cows. With a whispered word to her comrade, she sped away by a sheep-path that wound over against Maol-Gorm. Nial slowly advanced to the green hillock of Cnoc-na-shee. He had just flung himself wearily on the grassy slope, when he saw Torcall Cameron stoop and issue from his low doorway.

Màm-Gorm faced the way of the wind, sniffed the air with sensitive nostrils, and let his blind eyes feel the balm of the damp. Then he turned, and returned to his seat by the fire. Nial watched for an hour. The wind had a steady sough in it, and the clouds were lower, darker, more voluminously vast and swift, when Cameron came forth again.

It was this time that he had his staff in his hand, though no cap covered his tangled iron-gray hair.

Nial hoped he was right in believing that Màm-Gorm had come out merely to breathe the caller air; for the dwarf feared the reproach of Sorcha if he let the blind man wander along the perilous moorland, with wind and rain moving like ravenous hounds adown the heights.

When, however, he realized that Torcall Cameron was bent upon making his way to some distant spot, he had not the courage to check him, or even to make known his presence. There was a thunder-cloud on the man's face, oné that to Nial was far more sombre and terrifying than any overhead. When, with slow, hesitating steps, the blind man passed close to Cnoc-na-shee, he stopped for a few moments. Doubtless he was listening to the wind going through the pines, with a noise as of the flowing tide against shingly beaches; or, perhaps, to the scattered lowing and bleating of his sheep and cows. But Nial feared that, in some strange way, he had perceived him. He trembled, for he knew that "the father" was in one of his dark moods. Deep down in his heart, he dreaded the gaze of those sightless eyes more than anything else in the world: in his heart of hearts he was convinced that they saw, more awfully and searchingly because through a veil.

In his anxiety not to betray his presence, he ground his foot firmer into a heathy hollow, for he had slightly slipped when Cameron stopped. A pebble was dislodged, and made a slight noise.

The blind man lifted his head, startled.

"Is any one there?"

No answer. The wind sighed along the grass.

"Oona, are you there? Nial, is that you?"

Silence, but for a faint wind-rustle in the bracken.

"*Sst! Down, Luath, Fior!*"

But no collie barked or whined in response.

"Well, peace to your soul, and go hence."

But at last Torcall was convinced he was alone, for he heard the note of a yellow-hammer as it fed its mate, close by. With a sigh he moved on. As he passed within a few yards of Nial, the dwarf heard him muttering disconnected phrases: "Ochan-achone, tha

m'anam bruitc am chom! . . . ma tha sin an
dàn! . . . ma shìneas Dia mo làithean!"[1]

He waited till Cameron was some way ahead.
Then with light step, stealthy movement, and
furtive sidelong glances, he followed.

The first thin rain slanted along the wind.
The blind man paid no heed. Indeed, he now
walked swiftly and firmly along a sheep-path,
as though he were familiar with the way, or
had altogether forgotten his infirmity.

Out upon a bleak stretch of moor on one of
the higher slopes of Maol-Donn stood a cairn.
It was here, so rumor went, though none
knew for sure, that Torcall's wife, Marsail,
lay buried. It was known that she had perished in a snowstorm, and that he had insisted
on her burial where she was found; but when
the minister and the people came for her body,
they were told that she was already in the
mools, and that even now the stones of her
cairn were upon her.

Beside it was a tall flat slab of rock. It may
have been part of a Pictish or Druidic temple,
or its resemblance to a sacred stone may have
been accidental. It stood erect, one-third
embedded in the hillside.

To these Torcall Cameron now made his
way. At the Cairn he did not stop, neither

[1] "Alas, my soul is oppressed within me . . . if it be ordained . . if God prolong my days."

did he drop a stone or even a pebble upon it. When he reached the great rock, he leaned against it, and with folded arms stared sight-lessly across the strath to Tornideon, whose vast bulk rose sombre in the deepening gloom.

The wail of the wind momently increased. The rocks sweated, even where there was no rain falling.

Suddenly, over the high crest to the west, the Druim-nan-Damh, or Ridge of the Stags, there came a heavy rolling sound, as though a mass of boulders had fallen down the far side of Iolair.

This first muttering of the thunder aroused the dreamer. He started, checked some exclamation, and then, having stooped and groped till he found what he wanted, threw a small stone on Marsail's cairn.

Nial drew closer. A flash of lightning had frightened him. Thunder and lightning were to him as direct agents of a vengeful and irate Power, as they were to the priests and prophets of old.

The first loud crash filled the air; then ensued a splitting and rending as of a granite moun-tain, from whose depths vomited a prolonged howling and roaring as of monstrous beasts. The outcast crawled alongside the tall slab against which the man leaned, and gript a cor-ner with his hand.

When, his white face glimmering in the mirk, he looked up at Màm-Gorm, he shivered with a new dread.

The blind man stood erect, with arms up-raised and hands outspread. His face was lit as though a fire burned in his brain. Nial imagined that the dead eyes gleamed, as he had seen toadstools gleam in a dark cave: a dull phosphorescent light, horrible to look upon.

Again a wuthering roar, followed by a scythe-like whirlwind, with the sound of rain-tor-rents flooding the high corries and washing the windward precipices of Ben Iolair. Nial was about to speak, when he crouched back at the volley of words shouted savagely over his head.

"Oh, my Lord God, strike! Oh, let Death be upon me! Sorrow Thou hast given me, and I have not rebelled; grief Thou hast made my daily portion, and I have not rebuked Thee; but now that Thou hast made my day into a charnel-house and my bed into a grave, now that Thou hast brought before my blind eyes what no eyes may see and live, now that Thou hast set the Dead as a watch upon the living, — I cry to Thee, Enough!"

Nial shivered with awe and terror. He saw that a frenzy was upon the man whom he both loved and feared.

There was silence for many seconds. A

greenish streak of flame shot across the mountain, intolerably vivid. A sound as of mirthless laughter was drowned in an avalanche-
roar overhead. Out of the tumult, later, came
wild fragments of human shouting, —

"Let there be a duel between us then . . .
ay, Marsail, you may weep; ay, Fergus, you
may leap out of your shroud to be soul to soul
with me . . . what do I care for the hounds
of the night? . . . Call off thy hounds, O
Hunter! . . . Be the day between us, and the
night, O God; and the two noons, and the
darkness of the coming and the darkness of the
going; and the blood of the living, and the cor-
ruption of the dead; and the earth and the sea;
and the stars beneath the world, and the stars
above the world; and the friend of man that is
Time, and Thy friend that is Eternity . . .
for I *will* not, I *will* not, I *will* not . . . no,
though I perish forever and forever " . . . (and
at last, with a scream) . . . "Go Thy ways, O
God . . . Leave me, if Thou wilt not slay!
. . . I *will* not! I *will* not! I *will* not!"

When the next flash and thunder-blast had
hurtled and gone, Nial thought that Death had
indeed come. Then he heard a low whisper.

"What is it that I hear? Do the dead stir?
Marsail . . . Marsail . . . or . . . or . . . is
it *you*, Fergus, son of Fergus, son of Ian?"

Sick with fear, Nial sprang to his feet, seized one of the fallen hands in his own, and tried to lead Màm-Gorm away.

The blind man shook as a tuft of canna in a wind-eddy; white, too, as the canna, was his face.

His lips moved convulsively. At last, hoarse, choking, sobbing sounds came forth, and from these grew three or four words, —

" Is — it — *you*, Marsail ? "

Nial shrank appalled, but could not withdraw his hands.

" Is — it — *you*, Fergus Gilchrist ? "

Struggling to escape, he merely added to the paralyzing awe which held his captor.

"Who are you — what are you ? Are you the thing of the grave, the black guide I have heard of ? "

With a sudden jerk the dwarf freed himself. The next moment he bounded aside, then, without a glance behind him, fled.

Cameron sprang forward, but when he found that he had missed his grip he drew up again, and stood listening intently. If it was a spirit, it made a noise of running like a human; if it was a creature of the grave, it hurried back to no hollow near by; if it was Black Donald himself, Sir Diabhol had fled, affrighted.

Ah, the Cailliach! He had not thought of *her!* It might well be that the demon-woman had tried to snare him. If so, what, who, had saved him?

Dazed and sick he stood for a moment, because of a crash of a thunderbolt against a near height. The granite splintered like glass. In his mouth his palate shrank; his nerves strained, quivering.

Who, what, hurled that thunderbolt? Was it God? Was He answering his wild prayer?

If it were of God, why' had it not stricken him? Hark! A scream far off! Had the leaping Cailliach been slain by the lightning, as a flying man by the spear of his pursuer? Had God given him these things as signs,— these voices, — that awful touch as of human hands?

He bowed his head. Tears scalded the burning lids of his blind eyes. Suddenly he sank to his knees, and with outstretched arms repeated an ancient rune of his fathers, the Cry to Age, the Rann-an-h'Aoise:—

"O thou that on the hills and wastes of Night art Shepherd,
  Whose folds are flameless moons and icy planets,
  Whose darkling way is gloomed with ancient sorrows:
  Whose breath lies white as snow upon the olden,
  Whose sigh it is that furrows breasts grown milkless,
  Whose weariness is in the loins of man
  And is the barren stillness of the woman:

O thou whom all would 'scape and all must meet,
Thou that the Shadow art of Youth-Eternal,
The gloom that is the hush'd air of the Grave,
The sigh that is between last parted love,
The light for aye withdrawing from weary eyes,
The tide from stricken hearts forever ebbing !
O thou, the Elder Brother whom none loveth,
Whom all men hail with reverence or mocking,
Who broodeth on the peaks of herbless summits,
Yet dreamest in the eyes of babes and children :
Thou, Shadow of the Heart, the Brain, the Life,
Who art that dusk *What is* that is already *Has been,*
To thee this rune of the-fathers-to-the-sons
And of the sons to the sons, and mothers to new mothers —
To thee who art *Aois,*
To thee who art *Age !*

"Breathe thy frosty breath upon my hair, for I am weary ;
Lay thy frozen hand upon my bones that they support not,
Put thy chill upon the blood that it sustain not,
Place the crown of thy fulfilling on my forehead,
Throw the silence of thy spirit on my spirit,
Lay the balm and benediction of thy mercy
On the brain-throb and the heart-pulse and the life-spring —
For thy child that bows his head is weary,
For thy child that bows his head is weary.
I the shadow am that seeks the Darkness.
Age, that hath the face of Night unstarr'd and moonless,
Age, that doth extinguish star and planet,
Moon and sun and all the fiery worlds,
Give me now thy darkness and thy silence !

It was there, lying with his face in the wet
heather, that Sorcha´found her father. She
had seen Nial flying as for his life, and, from
behind the boulder where she was sheltering a
lamb, had sprung forward to stop him. But all

the elf-man saw was a woman's figure, —
perhaps the Cailliach who had already stolen
his soul, and now wanted his body in this
night of storm! With a scream he turned
aside, and dashed onward in his wild, ungainly
flight.

Sorcha's great eyes filled with amazement,
then with dread. What did it mean? Her
bosom heaved, the swell of the sudden tide at
her heart. More beautiful than any Fairy·
Woman that ever herded the deer or sang a
fatal song, she stood with one hand at her
breast, the color ebbing from her face, her
slim, firm body poised as an intent stag.

Slowly her gaze travelled back the way Nial
had come. In the gloom of storm she could
descry nothing, no one. If the Cailliach were
there, she was now invisible.

Again, an almost intolerably vivid flash of
blue-green light, out of a dazzling flame that
seemed to burst from the hills. The hollow
roar and crash that followed dazed her, but in
that moment's illumination she had seen the
cairn and the stannin' stane, and, beside them,
the figure of her father, apparently stricken and
fallen prone.

Without a thought of fear, either of the
storm or the evil spirit that might be roaming the hillside, she half ran, half clambered

upward, till she came upon her father lying low. In a moment she was by his side, and had lifted his head, drying his face with her dress, and kissing him, with a crooning as of a mother over her child.

He was not dead. For that she was thankful. She could feel the throb of his heart, and in his throat there was a sound as of sobbing breath.

"Father, father," she cried; then, whispering in his ear, "Father of me, father of me, oh, dear to my heart, all is well! I am Sorcha! There is no evil thing here. Come home! Come home!"

She felt the shiver that went over him. Then he sought with his hand, and clasped that which went to meet it.

"What is it, Sorcha? Where am I?"

"Ah, father, dear father, you are well now; arise, I will lead you home!"

"Home?"

"Yes; do you not hear the wind and the rain? *Ah — h —* !"

Again a bursting roar overhead, and the whole of Iolair a beacon of flame, whereon every boulder and crag stood out clear, as in brilliant moonlight.

"I remember! I remember!" Cameron cried, as he staggered to his feet. "Was it *you*, Sorcha, who took my hands a little ago, when — when — I was speaking to — to — Marsail? . . . "

The girl recoiled in horror. Marsail . . . her long dead mother!

"What is this thing that you say, O Torcall MacDiarmid?" she whispered, awe-struck.

"It is nothing. I was dreaming. Sorcha, I came here, dreaming of past days. Your mother lies below the cairn there. I was talking to her to ease my pain. I thought she might hear. And while I spoke, I felt hands clasp mine, and try to pull me down, — below the cairn, it may be! And then I fell into a horror, and the darkness came over my mind. And, suddenly, I knew that God spared me, though I had cursed Him, and I fell on my knees and cried the rune of Age, that is a rune of old forgotten among our people, and therewith I was heard, and my strength knew the Breath, and I fell as you found me."

"But, father, father, you are not in the dark way, — you are not old, for all the gray of your hair, — you are not going to die, and leave your Sorcha and Oona?"

"Would you have me live, *nic-chridhe?*"

Seldom did he speak to her thus, though often he called Oona his heart's dearic, and other loving names. The tears came to her eyes.

"Yes, yes, father! I would have you live.
I love you."

"My age is come upon me. I am weary."

"Not yet; not yet!"

"Do you not know the wisdom of old?—
S'mairg a dh'iarradh an aoise, Woe to him that
desireth extreme old age!"

"Come with me, dear! Come! The rain is
leaping at us. Come! You are cold and wet
and shivering!"

And so, at last, silent and weary, Torcall
Cameron toiled back against the tempest, and
neither he nor Sorcha saw, as they passed the
byre, a squat, misshapen figure, crouching
beside Odhar, the calving cow.

It was a night for the peat-glow. Outside,
the darkness was intense. The thunder-storm
had rolled heavily away, though the far hills
still held an echo. But a great wind had
arisen, and blew across the heights with a
sound like the trumpets of a mighty host.
From the forest came a vast, tumultuous sigh,
as of the moaning sea.

In the low room, where there was no light
save that of the peat-fire, upon which flamed
some dry pine-logs, Torcall Cameron sat brooding in the ingle. Opposite to him was Sorcha,
on a milking-stool, now stirring the porridge

in the pot at one side of the fire, now with clasped hands staring into the flames, dreaming of Alan, or of what she had that gloaming heard from her father and from Nial.

At dark she had gone to the byre, and, having found the dwarf, had soothed and entreated him, so that his dark mood passed, and he followed her, in furtive silence, into the room, where, unknowing of his advent, Màm-Gorm sat.

Only once had the blind man spoken since he had seated himself once again before the peats. It was to ask Sorcha if she thought that the person who took his hands by the cairn could have been Nial. An imploring glance from the outcast made her refrain from betrayal of his presence; of which she was glad, when, having replied that she was certain it was he, for she had seen him running down the hillside as though terrified by the lightning, her father broke into a muttered, savage curse.

At last Màm-Gorm slept. The fire-glow calmed the wrought face. The tangled iron-gray hair fell over his forehead. He looked strangely old; could it be, thought Sorcha, that his prayer had been heard, and that already the Shepherd had found this weary sheep? And yet, so strong was he, so tall and strong; strong as an aged pine on a headland. Surely, his ill was of the stricken heart only!

When his breathing came soft and even, she rose, lightly kissed his gray hair, with a tear for the pity of the old that is in the loving heart of the young, and then went out to the byre to see if Odhar was warm, and under no spell or evil, though her calf was not yet due.

As she went out, Oona slipped in. She was dry and flushed, for at the coming of the storm she had crept into the hayloft, and had there been lulled to sleep by the rush of the rain and the endless rising and falling sough of the wind. Nial made a sign of silence, so she came forward soundlessly. For a time she stared intently at the sleeper; then, seeing that Nial, who had crawled to her side, would not look at her, but sat blinking at the flame, she began to croon a song.

The sweet Gaelic words fell from her lips like soft rain in a wood. The room was filled with a low chime of music. Old strange chants or fugitive songs, one after the other, came fragmentarily to her lips; and the plaintive air of them was sometimes her own, sometimes what she had heard others sing, and once or twice old-world melodies, more ancient than the oldest pine-trees, older even that "the fallen stones" in the place on the south slope of

Iolair, called Teampull-nan-Anait, where a
thousand years ago none passed who could tell
who Anait was, or where her altar had been, or
who were her worshippers.

Once the door opened. Sorcha glanced
through the flame-lit dusk: a smile on her
face, sweet as the dream in her beautiful
eyes. The father asleep; Oona crooning
before the peats; Nial, quiet hound of Oona,
with dark eyes staring up at her from where
he lay on the floor: she need not fear to leave,
and go out to the roofed hay-room, where
Alan's arms yearned for her, where his heart
beat for her, where his lips were warm in the
dark, where the dear whisper of his voice was
the echo of the white song that clapped its
hands rejoicing in the sun-bower in the hollow
of her heart.

IV.

But, from that day, the gloom lay more heavily on Torcall Cameron even than of yore. Oona herself could hardly win speech from him. During the week of fine weather that followed the thunder-storm she was rarely at Màm-Gorm. The forest held her with its spell, though often she was on the heights with Murdo when he led the kye to the hill-pastures at sunrise, or with Sorcha at the milking of the cows at sundown.

During the noons, she sought — alone or with Nial — that white merle of which Sorcha had told her once, which had haunted her waking and sleeping dreams ever since. Whoever heard its song would be in fairyland for a thousand years, though the joy of that would be no more than a year and a day of mortal time. Whoever saw it might follow its flight, and for the seer of the white merle there would open wonder after wonder. The green spirits of the trees would come forth,

6

chanting low their murmurous rhyme; the souls of the flowers would steal hand-in-hand, from leaf-covert to leaf-covert, or dance in the golden light of the sunbeams; the singing of the birds, the crooning of the cushats, the hum of the wild-bee and the wood-wasp, the voices of all living things, from the low bleat of the fawn to the singing stir of the gnats by the pool or in the hollows, all would become clear as human speech, and would be sweet to hear.

Long, long ago that white merle had flown out of Eden. Its song has been in the world ever since, though few there are who hear it, knowing it for what it is, and none who has seen the flash of its white wings through the green-gloom of the living wood, — the sun-splashed, rain-drenched, mist-girt, storm-beat wood of human life.

But Oona watched for the white shimmer, for the magic song. She looked everywhere save where the white merle nested, — in the fair soul of her;' listened everywhere save where its secret song was, — in the music of her young life in heart and brain. Ah, the sweet song of it!

As for Nial, he crouched for hours at a time, lest by noon or dusk he might hear or see the magic bird. If only he could catch but a glimpse of the white merle, sure he would see his lost soul somewhere among the green spirits who, Oona said, would be seen coming out of the trees, which were their bodies. Neither did *he* know that there was one place where it rested often on a spray in its singing flight, a fugitive Hope; or that notes of its unreachable song pierced the gloom of his bitter pain.

Sorcha alone, only Sorcha, started at times as though she heard it; and in her dreams, and in the dreams of Alan, it sang, a white wonder on a golden bough, in the moonlight.

But for Torcall Cameron in his sorrow there was no white merle. Oona asked him once what its first notes were like.

"*Bron! Bron! Mo Bron!*" he answered, "mo bron, mo bron, ochone, arone! Doilghios orm' sa, tha mo chridhe briste!"[1]

Almost every afternoon he went out alone upon the heights, though never again by the cairn where Marsail lay. Sometimes he would sit on a boulder, brooding dark; at times Sorcha or Oona would descry him kneeling in the heather, often with fierce gestures, as he prayed wild prayers, — fragments of which the wind sometimes bore to the listener, who no more durst approach.

[1] "Grief, my grief! O grief, my grief, ochone, arone! Sorrow upon me, my heart is broken!"

Ever since that day by the cairn Nial had kept out of his way. Not without reason; for once, as the dwarf lay sleeping in the noon-heat, under the shadow of a rock, he was suddenly seized in an iron grip.

It was in vain for him to struggle. What he saw in the face of his captor gave him the courage of desperation.

"Let me go, Màm-Gorm!" he muttered, in a voice hoarse with passion. "Let me go. I am Nial of the woods."

"Ay, Nial of the woods! Spawn of the Evil One! Think you I don't know you to be the child of the Cailliach? You talk of your lost soul, poor fool! Your *lost* soul, you that never had and never will have a soul!"

"Let me go, Màm-Gorm!"

"Let you go, — and where will I be letting you go to, you that are no man, but only an elfish creature of the woods? Was it *you* that came out of the grave that day, — that day by the cairn?"

"And what will you do, Màm-Gorm?"

"What will I do? What will I do? By the blood on my soul, I will drive a stake through your body, so that no more shall you haunt the living!"

"Let me go, Torcall Cameron, in the name of God!"

The blind man relaxed his grip a little, which had become like a vice. The words brought a shock to his heart. He had never heard Nial call him by his name before; and if he were of demon birth, how could he say "an ainm an Athar"?

"Let me go, Torcall Cameron, or I will put a *rosad* upon you, a spell that no *sian* of Oona or Sorcha will save you from."

"*You*, you thing of the woods, *you* put a spell upon *me:* you who had my bread, and had my fire, and who would have died but for me? Ay, and you would put a spell upon me! And what would that *rosad* be like now, from you that have never consorted with men, and have learned nothing save from the lassie Oona?"

"When I was with the children of the wind," Nial began, to be interrupted at once by his captor, who muttered, "Ah, the gypsies! I forgot —" and grew grave, as with the shadow of a fear.

"When I was with the children of the wind, Màm-Gorm, I learned some things that even you may not know. And in the woods I have learned that which no man knows. And if I put the evil upon you, you will die slowly, year by year, from the brain that is behind your eyes to the last bones of your feet!"

Cameron shuddered.

"It may be so.   God forgive me any way.
You have done me no harm.   But look you,
Nial of the woods, keep out of my way when I
wander abroad — and let me hear no more of
your spells.   There, you are free to go.   Yet
even now that my hand is off you, I long to
make sure that you are not the thing that came
out of the cairn."

With a dark, vengeful face the elf-man moved
out of reach; then he whispered in a slow,
meaning way,—

"I am going, for I see Marsail coming down
the hill from the cairn, and with her is a man—"

"A man!   A man!" shouted Cameron, trembling as in an ague.   "Who is the man?   What
is he like?   Give me your hand, Nial, give me
your hand, for the love of God!"

"He is tall and fair, and dripping wet, with
his hair lank about his head, with the water
in it."

Ah, he had his revenge now!   Màm-Gorm
gave a low moan, and sank to his knees.
There he cowered, muttering incoherently.

"Nial," he whispered hoarsely at last, "Nial,
Nial, do they come this way — Marsail and —
and — the man who is dripping wet?"

The dwarf raised his head and stared about
him.   He was tempted to make his late tor-

mentor suffer but the brute heart of the soul-less man was melted because of the agony of one of the lords of life.

"I see no one now, Màm-Gorm."

"No one — *no one?*"

"No."

"Are you sure, Nial?"

"I am sure."

"Give me your hand."

"You will do me no hurt?"

"On my soul!"

Nial slowly advanced, took the outstretched hand in his, and helped the trembling man to rise.

"Nial, tell me this thing. Have you seen these — these — these *two* before this?"

"I have never seen the woman."

"Then how do you know it was Marsail, who is dead years and years and years agone?"

"Is it forgetting you are that when I was a child I saw her body, on the day of the snow?"

There was a pause, wherein the questioner brooded darkly. At last, in a low, strained voice, he asked, —

"Have you ever seen the man?"

"No."

"Do you know who he was?"

"No."

"Can you guess who he was?"

Silence.

"Speak, Nial!"

Silence.

"Speak, Nial, whom I have fathered."

"He was dripping wet, as though, as though—"

"Well?"

"*As though he had fallen into the Linn o' Mairg.*"

A savage spasm came into Cameron's face. The nails of his fingers drew blood in the prisoned hand, which was snatched away as Nial again moved out of reach.

"I will lay my curse upon you, you evil beast!" Cameron shouted hoarsely,—"Dhonas's a dholas ort!—Bas dunach ort!—Ay, ay, Nial the Soulless, son of the demon-woman, God against thee and in thy face, drowning on sea and burning on land, a stake of the whitethorn between thy heart and the pit of thy belly!"[1]

Of the few curses he knew, none seemed

---

[1] "Dhonas's a dholas ort"—"Bas dunach ort:" *i. e.* Evil and sorrow to you! . . . A death of woe be yours! "God against thee, etc.": this dreadful and dreaded anathema runs in the Gaelic—"Dia ad aghaidh's ad aodann, bathadh air muir is losgadh air tir, crogan sgithhich eadar do chridhe's t'airnean:" from which it will be seen, by those who know Gaelic, that I have not translated literally either "crogan" or "airnean."

to Nial so terrible, so mysterious, so straight
upon life out of Death, as that conveyed by the
two words, "Marbh'asg ort!"

He waited till the fury of the man was spent.
Then, frowning darkly, with his red bloodshot
eyes agleam, he muttered "*Marbh' asg ort!* . . .
Your death-wrappings be about you!" So
low was his voice that it fell unheeded.

Cameron turned his sightless eyes upon
him. He shivered. The blindness of his
king hurt him as a searing pain.

"What was the thing you said, Nial of the
brutes?"

With a great effort the bitter word was
slain ere it was spoken. The voice that came
from that wild fantastic woodland thing, with
its shaggy peaked head, its faun-like ears,
its rude, misshapen body, was ever harsh
as a branch grating in the wind; but now
it was gentle. Tears that were unshed soft-
ened it. The grief of the pariah was its
benediction.

"Màm-Gorm, my father, the thing I said
was a bitter thing out of Nial the herd; but
this thing that I say to you is by poor Nial
of the brutes, and that is, *God preserve you.*
. . . *ay, gu'n gleidheadh Dia thu, Torcall-mo-
maighstir!*"

And with that the brute turned from the

man who had cursed him, and with slow steps and bent head made his way across the hillside, till he entered the forest, whence he came not for three days, and where none, not even Oona, saw him.

It may be that he had heard at last the song of the White Merle.

V.

So the weeks went till the coming of the
season that, because of the heats and of the
drought, is called the month of the hanging
of the dog's mouth.[1]

Great heat, with many thunders, had prevailed. For nine days at the beginning of July
the rain poured, — or ceased only to let rainbows come and go upon the gleaming hills.
During this time Oona and the blind man at
Màm-Gorm were much together. A change
had come upon the child. She looked at her
foster-father often, with a wistful gaze. Something puzzled her. In the air, some vague
trouble moved like a vanishing shadow. Of
Nial she saw little. Now and again she heard
his signal in the forest, and answered it:
sometimes, at dawn or dusk, coming upon
him on the hillside, sitting solitary on some
isolated boulder, or crouching by a pool, and

[1] *Mios crochaidh nan con.* This month is the period from
the middle of July till the middle of August.

staring intently into its depths. But he would
not come across the *airidh*. No one knew
how he lived. Once or twice Murdo, the
shepherd, gave him to eat; and, every morning and night, Oona put a small crock of porridge and oat-cakes, or other food, in a place
where the vagrant could have it if he willed,
— and thrice, at least, she found it empty.
On the few moonlit nights she fancied she
saw a pale misty column of thin smoke rise
above the pines.

Still more was she troubled about Sorcha.
Her beautiful sister had grown even lovelier
to look upon, but there was a new look in her
eyes, a new hush in her voice. She shep-
herded on the mountain as one in a trance; as
one in a dream she moved about the house.
At night, in her sleep, she sighed often, and
moaned gently; and once, turning and finding
Oona by her, she put her arms round the child,
and, sleeping still, whispered, "*Ah, heart of
my heart, joy of my joy!*"

She knew that Sorcha and Alan Gilchrist
loved each other. She knew, also, that this
was why Alan could never come to Màm-
Gorm, for her foster-father had laid his ban
upon their love. But what did this love
mean? What, she pondered vaguely, did this
tragic silence, this tragic yet happy silence,

hide? "I know now," she said one day to
Sorcha, at the coming home of the kye, "I
know now why it is that Alan, when he meets
you in the gloaming by the byre, or in the
hay-shed, or down in the strath by the Mairg
Water, calls you 'Dream.'"

Sorcha was startled, and the beautiful face
flushed at the knowledge that she had been
seen at these secret meetings with Alan.
Oona's unconsciousness of any cause of em-
barrassment, however, reassured her.

"So you have seen us, Oona my flower?
Well, see to it that you say nothing of this
to father, or to any one. And, Oona, my
bonnie, how do you know he — Alan — calls
me 'Dream,' and what do you mean by saying
you know now what that means?"

"I heard him call you so that moonlight
night last week, when you came hand in hand
through the wood. He called you Sunshine,
Joy, and then Dream; and you said that
'Dream' was best, for it was the name he
gave you '*that* day' . . . Sorcha!"

"Yes, birdeen."

"What was '*that* day'?"

The girl turned her face aside, because of
the flame in it; but the flush was in the white
neck as well, and the child laughed.

"Ah, it was when he first kissed you!"

"Yes, dear," Sorcha answered, flushing again; "yes, it must have been then."

"Sorcha, tell me, do you love him very much?"

"Yes. More than I can tell you, my sunbeam. When you are a woman you will understand."

"When I am a woman I am going to marry Nial."

"Nial!"

"Yes. No one will love him, because he has no soul ; but *I* love him, and will marry him. Half of my soul will then be his."

"Is that so, then? Sure 't is a south wind for Nial! And where will you live, Oona-my-heart?"

"The White Merle will show us the way."

"Ah, I see, it is a fairy tale. Well . . . Oona, I will tell you a secret. *I* have heard the song of the White Merle!"

The child's eyes grew big with wonder and excitement.

"When? Where? Was it where the old yews are in the Upper Strath?"

"It was now here and now there."

"But when, when?"

"Whenever Alan called me ' Dream,' and the other names, I heard the song of the White Merle."

"Ah, it is you that I envy! Sorcha, do you think that if Nial called me beautiful names, I should hear it too?" .

"I fear not, dearie . . . *not yet.* Perhaps — perhaps if *you* called *Nial* those beautiful names, *he* would hear the song."

"Then I will."

"No, not yet, Bonnikin. You will only harm Nial. But now run away. Father will be seeking you."

"Ah, and who will be seeking *you?*" cried Oona, as she danced away, laughing. "Ah, 't is a good name, *Dream;* for you are always dreaming in your eyes now, Sorcha!"

Yet day by day thereafter the child laughed less blithely. There was a shadow about her foster-father. It held her spell-bound. Never had she been so long away from the woods before, never before had she been so long indoors. She was glad to be with the blind man, and to take his hand when he went out to stride sometimes for miles along the rough ways of the hills. She talked much to him about the White Merle, and the "guid-folk," and the quiet people; sometimes of Nial, and of the strange things he saw and heard, and how the birds and beasts would come to him, and how he harmed none, nor they him.

Sometimes she asked about the Cailliach, or about the wind-spirits; or strange questions about the people of the strath, glimpses of whom she had occasionally, and for whom, particularly for the black-garbed minister, she did not conceal her contempt and dislike. Sometimes she sang; and that was what the blind man liked best. Once only she spoke of Alan: how she thought that Christ must be like him, so fair to see was he; how she loved his low voice and soft touch and grave sweet eyes.

But she saw at once that no good would come out of any mention of that name. Her foster-father grew moodily taciturn; and when, after a long silence, he spoke, it was to ask her, in a harsh voice, if she had ever broken his command, and climbed the opposite slopes of Tornideon.

"Never, father."

"And have you ever sought the woman Anabal, that is mother of Alan?"

"No."

He seemed satisfied, and asked nothing further. But as for Oona, she brooded over this more and more, and wondered more and more because of the ban upon Alan, and because of the feud between Torcall Cameron in his loneliness on Iolair and Anabal Gilchrist in her loneliness on Tornideon.

The first day of August came with settled weather and almost tropic heat.

All that day Torcall Cameron had been strangely restless. If Oona left him for more than a few moments he grew impatient, and then angry. Again and again she begged him to come into the green shadowy woods, or even to climb to the Ridge of the Stags on Iolair; but he would not. At last, weary with the heat and the long blank hours, weary, too, with Oona's importunities, and not wholly unwilling to humor her for his own sake, he let her take his hand and lead him forth at her will.

Sorcha alone knew that, for some reason which she never fathomed, her father's " black day" was this first day of August. Year after year his "dubhachas," his gloom, came upon him with that dawn, so that he would have word with none. She knew, too, that when the dark day was gone, her father was better for weeks thereafter, and sometimes smiled and laughed like other men.

The night before had been an ill passing of July. Murdo, the shepherd, had come in, his face white. As he had come down the mountain he had heard a wild and beautiful singing, and had descried a herd of deer being driven with the wind, keeping close together. He had

not seen the demon-woman, for he had turned his
head away, and muttered a *sian* to keep the evil
of her from coming about him like a snake.
But he thought the wind brought some of the
words of her song to him, and they were of
death and the grave. Then, muttering, "Glacar
iad's na innleachdan a dhealbh iad,"—Let them
be taken in the devices they have imagined, —
he had fled. Later, Oona came with a strange
story from Nial. He had been crossing the
highland behind Màm-Gorm, and had seen two
men and two women walking silently with
bowed heads. One man was tall and dripping
wet, as though he had come out of water, and
his lank hair hung adown his face. The other
man was Màm-Gorm himself. The faces of the
others he could not see; but one woman was
tall and gaunt, with wild straggling gray hair, —
a woman like Anabal Gilchrist on Tornideon.
He heard only one word spoken, and that was
when Màm-Gorm stopped, looked at the house,
and said, " C'aite am bheil an eilidriom?" [1]

"What is an *eilidriom*, Sorcha?" Oona had
added. To which her sister had replied that

[1] "Where is the hearse?" *Eilidriom* (pronounced like *à-ee-drèm*) is used in Skye and the isles, rarely if ever on the main-
land. *Snaoimh* (bier) is the common word, though when a
hearse is actually meant it is alluded to as the *carbad-mhàrbh*
"the death-chariot."

she did not know, and that she was to say nothing of this in the house.

" And what then, Oona? "

Nial, the child resumed, had heard no more.
But when he turned and looked towards the
strath he saw nine men moving away from
Màm-Gorm, carrying in their midst a long black
box. When he glanced back, the four wayfarers he had seen had disappeared.

Yet, as Sorcha knew, her father had not
stirred from the house that day. Nothing of
what Murdo or Nial had šeen came to his ears
— of that she was heedful. But suddenly, while
they were eating the porridge, Oona asked her
foster-father what an " eilidriom " was.

⁻ Cameron sprang to his feet, pale as death, and
shaking, with the milk that he had spilt from
the mug in his hand running down his breast,
as though his life-blood were pouring from him,
white too with fear.

" *What is that you say, Oona?* " he cried
hoarsely; "what is that you say? *Do you see a
carbad-mhàrbh — at the door — coming here?* "

" No — no — " murmured the child, terrified.

" Then how do you know that word for it?
Who told it to you? I have not heard it said
for years. No man uses it in this country. I
have not heard it since — since Marsail died —
and then it was from — from the people yonder

on Tornideon, for Anabal Gilchrist was of the isles."

But here Sorcha had interposed, and said that O'ona had picked it up in some way, in one of the old runes told her by Murdo, no doubt.

For the rest of that night Torcall Cameron only once opened his lips, and that not at the covering of the peats, or when Sorcha sang one of the sweet *orain spioradail* he loved so well, after she had read a while in the Book of Peace. It was when she came to him after he had lain down in his bed, and kissed him, and let her flooding tears fall warm upon his blind up-staring eyes; then he pulled her head closer, and whispered, " Sorcha, Sorcha, my soul swims in mist."

It was a night of beauty, and still. All slept. But towards dawn a voice arose in the corries. From height to height it went, and the long wail of it swept past the green *airidh* of Màm-Gorm and wandered sobbing through the forest. Then all was still again. The dawn that came soon after was of pale gold and faintest wild-rose. Peace was in the heaven.

But with that sudden passing wail, so often heard on the mountains when there is not a cloud in the sky, and when, far and near, not a branch sways, and the gnats dance in long columns perpendicularly, without drifting this way or that, — with that voice out of the hills, Torcall awoke.

When Sorcha arose she heard him moaning. Wearily she wondered what this fateful date meant, — this dreaded first day of the eighth month. When she went to him, he said no other word than this: " I have heard the lamentable cry of death."

" The cry of death?" she repeated questioningly.

" Ay, truly, the lamentation of the demon-women mourning for the dead."

So it was that all that day Torcall Cameron had been as a man in an ill dream, weary of the long hours, yet dreading the passing of them into the shadow. So, too, it was that at the last he went forth with Oona.

At first they wandered into the forest; but here Torcall was never at ease, and so after a time they strolled hand in hand from glade to glade, till the sound of Mairg Water came soothing-cool through the heat.

The peace and utter quietude lay as balm upon the weary man. He grew drowsy at last, as his trouble seemed to lift from him. More than once he would have stopped and thrown himself on the ground, content to stir no further; but Oona urged him to come on to where the river ran through shelving ledges with a singing sound, and nothing else was to be heard but the whisper of the silver birches and the thin green reeds.

The crooning of the cushats was in his ears. Sweet it was to have that soft touch of sound after the lamentable cry of the hills, that mourning cry now dulled, so that it was there only as a shadow in a darkened room.

He was glad when the breath of the water came upon his face, and he could sit down among the bracken and fragrant gale, and do no more than listen idly to the passage of the water. The whispering water, the scarce audible susurrus of faintly stirred leaves overhead, the singing of the gnats, the low, incessant croon of the cushats, — these were all the sounds to hear. Not a breath of wind moved in the pinewood, so that it gave not even that vast slow suspiration which may be heard in forests once or twice between sunrise and sundown even on stillest days. All the birds were still, though few sang even at daybreak in that season of the young brood. Over the reaches of the water the swallows skimmed, hawking silently.

An hour passed. Thinking that he slept, and weary of sitting still so long, Oona rose and slipped away. At first, she went to a great yew that towered near the fringe of the forest, to see

if the wood-doves she had heard crooning there
had fallen asleep, for now they no longer made
their croodling moan. Then, having espied
them, sitting close with fluffed plumage and
drooping wings, as they drowsed in the warm
shadow, she peered here and there for the nest
of a shrew-mouse, for often she had heard there-
abouts the patter of the wild mice in days of
drought.

Her quest led her on and on. A sudden
splash made her look at the narrow river. A
grilse had leapt half out of the clear amber-
brown water, and missed the dragon-fly which
had been poising its arrow-flight close to a
wreath of circling foam. The tumult of the
Linn, a score of yards beyond her, was pleasant
in her ears. She forgot the shrew-mice, and
thought only of the great salmon that Nial
declared slept or lay waiting night and day
under a ledge at the bottom of the Linn. Yes,
she would steal across the rocks, and creep in
among the boulders, and lie along the lowest
ledge that sloped to the seething hollow, whose
black depths, and the deafening noise of whose
tumult, had ever an irresistible fascination for
her.

She seemed like a water-sprite herself as she
stood on a high rock, at a place where the
ledges sloped sheer into a crevice, at the bot-

tom of which a snake of brown water writhed through holes and crannies till it leapt out into a back eddy of the river whence it came. She had plucked a branch of rowan-berries, some still green or ruddy brown, but others already kissed into flame by the sun. This she waved slowly to and fro before her, partly to keep the midges away, partly because the rhythm of the running water was flowing through her brain, and so along all the nerves of her body. The sunflood beat full upon her. Her short, ragged, scanty dress glowed like a chestnut-husk in the sunlight; in the hot yellow sunshine the tanned skin of her legs and feet gleamed ivory white. With parted lips and shining eyes she stood, intent, transfigured.

Suddenly she started. A look of curiosity, of astonishment, came into her eyes.

What, she wondered, was that unfamiliar object lying in a ferny hollow of the rocks which formed the bridge of Mairg Water, whence the stream fell in a rushing cataract into the Linn? A human figure, clearly; a woman, too. Who could she be? Was she alive or dead? Was it Sorcha? No. Could it be one of the fairy-women of whom she had heard so often; the Cailliach, of whom she had been told so many tales; or that green-clad, yellow-scarfed, mysterious Bandruidh, the sorceress who won the souls

out of grown men, and whose glance was fateful
as a kelpie's? A kelpie's! Ah, was this indeed
not the kelpie of the Linn o' Mairg, lying there
in wait for her; or might it be in truth the kelpie, yet only asleep there in the great heat? If
so, now was the time to espy it, and perhaps
steal or find a hair of its head, which, wound
about the third finger of her left hand, would
make her a princess among the secret people,
and enable her to know what no one in the
whole strath or the greater strath of the world
beyond would know, to see what no one would
see.

These were the thoughts which passed through
her mind, while her blue eyes gazed unwaveringly at the woman, dead or asleep.

At last, slowly and with careful heed, she
drew nearer and nearer. When still many yards
away she recognized the sleeper, whose deep
regular breathing reassured her. It was Anabal Gilchrist, the mother of Alan, the woman
banned to her and Sorcha by their father as
though she were accursed. True to her word,
Oona had never been at Ardoch-beag, the widow
Anabal's farm; but several times she had caught
a glimpse of the solitary woman, and now knew
her at the first glance. Once, more than two
years back, she had been luring trout one evening in the Mairg Water, near Ardoch ford, and

had been startled by the sudden appearance of a woman who had seized her in her arms, and kissed her over and over, sobbing convulsively the while. The woman had drawn her plaid over her head, and what with this and the dusk and her fear, Oona had not time to discover who it was. Later, she was convinced that it was no other than the mother of Alan.

When she saw her now before her, she stood hesitatingly. She felt drawn to this sad-faced woman who had once snatched her in the dusk and covered her face with kisses; but she was still more attracted by the mystery which enveloped her.

It was only a quarrel, Sorcha had told her; and often she had heard her sister say that if only her father and Anabal would meet, all might be explained. In a flash an idea came into the child's mind. The thought sent the blood leaping from her heart. Her eyes shone.

Two motives impelled Oona. Neither was of itself, but one was interwrought with the other. The love of mischief, with her innate audacity and fearlessness, urged her to place her foster-father in the last place in the world where he would fain be; but, also, something in her heart pleaded for the quiet bringing together, in that hushed and beautiful sun-going, of these two bitter haters.

Yes, she would do it, though she knew that her foster-father's wrath might fall heavily upon her. If — if only Sorcha — no, she did not care, she would do it. After all, no harm would come of it. She would watch, and if the woman rose and went away, she would come back and take her foster-father's hand and lead him home again.

Though the woman slept, overcome with weariness, why was it that a trouble of deep sorrow still lay upon her face, as the trouble of waters even after the sea-wind has died into the blue calm of the air? The tears were still wet upon the hand that lay across her breast; why had they fallen? The child stood awhile, brooding. What did it mean? Slowly she glanced about her. No one was visible. It was clear that by the way the woman lay she had not fallen.

At that moment Oona noticed that Torcall had slipped a little, because of the slope whereon he had lain. Drowsily he was feeling about him for an easier rest.

Like a hare, as swift and as soundlessly, she made her way to him.

" Rise, father," she whispered; " come further up the stream. It is pleasanter there."

For nights Torcall Cameron had had little or no sleep.

Weary with these long, long hours; weary

with his fasting and his restless idleness; weary
with the windless heat; and, above all, weary of
his own thoughts and of himself, he resigned
himself gladly into Oona's hands.

Even as he walked he swayed. Sleep was so
heavy upon him that the roar of the waters of
the Linn came to him no loudlier than as the
muffled song and humming rhythm of the
stream itself.

Gently, with her heart beating the while, the
child led the blind man to the place where the
woman Anabal, after long weeping, had fallen
into deep slumber. He lay down like a child.
The noise of the rushing waters lulled him, the
ancientest, sweetest cradle-song in all the wide
green world. If he heard at all the breathing
of the sleeping woman, no other thought could
have come to him than that it was Oona.

She stared down at them with awe-struck
eyes. What was this unthinkable terror that
shook her like a leaf? For a moment she con-
quered her fear, a fear so vague, and of the soul
only, that she did not know she was afraid,
though the nerves in her body leapt to the
breath of it.

The tears came into her eyes. Yellow was
the light that fell upon the tangled iron-gray
hair of the weary sleeper at her feet; yellow as
yellow flowers was the gleam upon the brown-
gray tresses of the weary sleeper by his side.

The hand of the woman moved. Out of the
sun-glow the arm crept like a snake; then it lay
still in the shadow betwixt the two, who slumbered unheeding.

Oona knew not why she did it, or even what
she did; but with a touch, light almost as the
warm sunbeam itself, she guided the .hand of
Anabal towards that of Torcall. As two ships
draw together on a calm sea, though far apart,
so the hands of these two, who had not spoken
one with the other for weary years, slipped at
last side by side. The man stirred a moment,
smiled, and gently clasped the hand in his.

Then, when all was well, Oona shivered with
actual dread. What if they should die so?
What if they were already dead? Once more
she fought back this terrifying emotion. How
quiet they seemed! Sweet is the gray sleep of
the old.

" *Tha iad rèidha nis,*" she sighed rather than
whispered; " they are at peace now."

But now no longer could she stay. Like a
fawn, after she had crept back upon the grassy
ledges, she leapt from boulder to boulder. Soon
she was at the verge of the forest. Inexplicable
fear drove her like a whip. Minute after minute passed, and still she fled as though pursued.
Nearly a mile had she gone before she stopped,
only to fling herself into the bracken in a shel-

tered place, a kind of cave formed by the gigantic roots of a fallen pine-tree, long years ago wrenched away like a reed and stricken to the ground. There, sobbing at she knew not what, she cried herself to sleep at last. When the dark came, her slumber was unbroken. A solitary moonbeam that made its way through the dense covert to where she slept, lay upon her feet, upon her slow-moving breast, upon the white flower of her face, upon the out-spread tangle of her hair, which it clothed with fugitive pale gold. No vision of ill disturbed her. Once only she stirred as, in dreamland, she thought she heard the song of the White Merle.

VI.

WHEN the gloaming fell upon the Linn o'
Mairg, Anabal stirred. The churr of a fern-
owl echoed in her ear, and dimly she awoke to
the knowledge that it was late. But where
was she? She had dreamed a pleasant dream.
Hand in hand, — even now, she thought, — hand
in hand even now were she and Fergus, — Fergus
so long dead, and never come again to put his
lips against the pain in her heart.

After all, was it a dream? Or, rather, was
not all that weary past a dream? She would
not open her eyes. She would press the hand
that clasped hers, then she would know.

Ah, the joy and the pain of it! It was Fergus
indeed! She had moved her hand and pressed
his, and the pressure had been returned — faintly
and slowly, as though in sleep, yet still returned!
But where was she? That noise of waters all
about her, that ceaseless surge and splash, the
smell of the rushing water, the cool spray upon
· her face, — was this not indeed the Linn o'
Mairg, where, late that afternoon, she had
fallen asleep?

Now at last it was clear. Yes, she was at the Linn o' Mairg. But the time of her mourning was over, and her evil was no more anywhere in the blue sky or in the green earth, for Fergus had come to her.

In this hour of death she must tell him all. She would not open her eyes yet awhile. She, of the living, might not be able to look on *that* of the dead. And first, moreover, she must speak.

"*Fergus!*"

No sound came from the sleeper by her side. She imagined that his hand quivered, but she did not know for sure.

"*Fergus!*"

Ah, now he was awake from his death-sleep, for she heard his breath come quick and hard. The hand she held in hers shuddered as with palsy.

"Ah, cold hand of my heart," she murmured, raising it, chafing it the while, and putting it to her lips at last.

"Ah, cold hand out of the grave! Often have I felt it at my heart! Fergus, dear to me, Fergus, Fergus! Ah, one word to me, one word to me!"

Still no whisper from the man beside her. She could hear the shuddering breath of him.

"Fergus, I must speak! If the dead know

aught, lang syne you must have known I knew
nothing of the evil deed done upon you. But
oh, my man, my man, I had loved Torcall before
I loved *you !* Fergus, listen! Do not draw
away from me! Do not rise! Fergus, Fergus,
I *must* tell you all! "

"*Speak !* "

Awe came upon her, as a sudden darkness at
noon. The dead had spoken. The life in her
body tore at the gateway of the heart. The
voice was human, hoarse and low as it was.
Almost she had courage. Once more that low,
hoarse mandate came. The sound shuddered
through the dark upon her ear.

"*Speak !*".

"Be not too hard upon me, Fergus! I loved
him, though not as he loved me. I never for-
gave him because that in his anger he married
Marsàil. But when I was to marry you, whom
I loved as I had never loved him — "

Here the sobbing woman stopped a moment
because of the fierce grip upon her hand, then,
panting, resumed, —

" . . . Then, as God knows my soul, I put him
out of my heart. But the wild beast in him arose
and rent him. He went to and fro, mad because
of his lust of me. Then the day came when,
in my weakness and loneliness, he had his will of
me. For days after that I did not see him.

8

Then the spell of the sin fell upon me, and it was sweet — sweet for a brief while was that evil and accursed dream! Then it was that you came back from the fishing among the isles, to this place where your father lived, and where I was, because of the mother that bore me, and is long dead, God be praised! And when you married me, Fergus, the child that is Oona was already within me, God shaping that burden there underneath my heart till every pulse beat heavy with it! And now you know the thing that has eaten at my life all these weary years."

No sound, save the constrained sobbing breath of him who listened.

"*Look!*" he whispered at last.

Slowly Anabal opened her eyes. In the misty dusk she could see the white sheen of the flying water, but not the face of her beloved. The dark figure was there, clothed as in life. Taller he seemed, and broader; but sure, Fergus — sure, Fergus. Who but he, with those eyes of love and longing burning upon her out of the night!

"*Anabal!*"

O God, the agony of it! The voice was even as the voice of Torcall, the man who had sown her womb with the seed of sin, and had reaped blindness and sorrow all the years of his life. Bitter the mockery of this thing.

"Fergus! Fergus! Heart o' me, husband!"

"*Anabal!*"

With a scream she sprang to her feet. She swayed as one drunken. The man saw it, though he was blind —

"Back! back! back!" she cried, groping blankly with outstretched arms. "Back, if you be a phantom out o' hell! Back, if you be the Fiend himself! Back, Fergus, back, if dead ye be, and are here but to mock me. Back! back! back! Torcall Cameron! Back, man, back! I am gray, gray, withered, gray and old. . . . *Ah, my God!*"

He had leapt upon her as a wolf leaps. She was in his grasp, and the strength in her was as melting snow.

"Anabal! God hears me. I dare not lie to you, I, who am blind — "

"Torcall Cameron, as God is my witness, I saw your face in his dead eyes."

The man groaned; then, as though weary, spoke once again.

"I have sworn. I have not lied. Fergus slipped and fell, I not touching him or near him at the time. I tried to catch him as he fell, but the Mairg Water was in spate, and it was useless. He came out at the Kelpie's Pool. He was not quite dead, and I looked into his eyes ere the veils came on."

Still no word.   Only that dread silence.

" Anabal ! "

" Anabal !   Let all this misery be at an end.
Sorrow has aged us both.   But I have loved
you ever.   I love you now.   Woman, woman,
you were mine, all of you, all of you, mine
to the leaping body, to the beating heart, to
the shaking soul ! — mine — mine — before ever
he touched you !   Mine you were before ever
I put my sin upon you; mine you have been
ever since, and ever sh— "

" Torcall ! "

" I hear."

" Who brought you hither, this night of all
nights ? "

" Oona."

No sooner had he spoken the name than a
cry escaped his lips, mate of that which burst
from hers.

" Go, go !   Man, devil, murderer, madman,
go, go ! " and, screaming thus, with a fierce
struggle Anabal Gilchrist strove to escape from
the grip that held her.

" Anabal ! Anabal !   At least do not send me
to my death !   I am blind.   Lead me home.
Put me hence, and through the wood.   I am
blind, and the night lives with terrors for me ! "

For a moment the woman was about to yield.
A long tress of her gray-brown hair fell upon

his hand, and he grasped it as a drowning man
at a rope. Then she saw, or believed that she
saw, a look in his face that maddened her.

" *Never*, so help me God ! "

Without a word, he was upon her. He had
her in his arms, and was laughing low, horribly,
mirthlessly.

" I will never let you go, Anabal ! . . . I have
waited long. . . . You are mine, and no one
else's. . . . Mine you were, mine you are, mine
you 'll be till the Last Day and forevermore ! "

She felt one arm slacken, and his hand seek
hers. Before she realized what he did, he had
snatched the wedding-ring from her finger and
thrown it into the Linn.

Once more he laughed.

" Anabal ! Anabal ! . . . Anabal, my Joy ! I
love you . . . I love you . . . I love you. All
the youth of my life is upon me again. I am
blind, but I see you as on the day when you
quickened with new life. Dear, O my dear,
heart of me, joy of me ! Anabal, listen ! I am
Torcall ! All is forgotten ; all the weary years
are gone. Sweetheart, this is my heart against
your heart ! *Ah — h — h !* "

He had seized her, and the flames of his
kisses scorched her face. Between his parting,
sobbing cries, and her choking breath, he buried
his face in her hair, heedless of the gray blight

upon that yellow corn, and bruised that quivering body, whose flesh was still so warm, so firm,
young long after the breath of age on the hair,
in the eyes.

Then she gathered the strength that was in
her. With a fierce blow she made him reel, so
that he nigh slipped and fell.

" Murderer ! "

A blank silence came upon them. Around,
the rush of the water: swift-sighing it seethed
beyond, with hollow roar and surge, in the Linn
below where they stood. Over the forest lay a
faint yellow bloom, the moon shining upon it
from behind Ben Iolair. A fern-owl churred its
love-cry through the warm fragrant night. A
thin, impalpable mist obscured the few stars that
shone, but the splintered lance-rays of them
glistered this faint exhalation of the earth.

When the man spoke, his voice was as though
frozen.

" It is a lie."

" No lie is it, Torcall Cameron; for I see the
naked truth in your soul."

" It is a lie."

" Where is my man, where is my man Fergus,
whom you slew ? "

" I slew him not."

" Liar! liar! Even here, on this very spot,
on this very night years agone, he came upon
his death at your hand ! "

"Listen! I heard *you;* now hearken to *me.* . . . On that night, but before it was dark, we met, here. It is true. True also that there was fear and hate between us. But as God hears me, as God sees me, as God hath stricken me blind and gloomed the bitter life of me, I did not put his death upon him."

"Anabal!"

Her breath came hot against his face.

"Anabal!"

No word, no sign. He knew by the passage of her breath that she looked now this way and now that: behind him, beside, beyond.

She saw that they were standing now on the extreme of the slippery ledge that overhung the seething depths. No longer did she make any attempt to resist him. Death called out of the pool. She made no effort to save either him or herself.

"Anabal!"

Mechanically she moved her arms as though to free herself. She felt his hold slacken.

"Anabal! Do you yield?"

"I yield."

Mechanically, again, she leaned forward and kissed him on the breast. The next moment his foot slipped. He reeled, staggered wildly.

' Anabal snatched her arm away.

Again he slipped and fell forward. He was

now on the very edge of the ledge. His hand
fell upon one of her feet. She stooped to push
aside his arm. He raised it, caught at something, gave a wild cry, and shot into the dark,
with heavy plunge and splash.

In the moonshine, — for the yellow bloom
had now expanded into a flood of rippling gold,
— she saw the black mass of his body whirled
to and fro. Once the white face was turned to
her, — a blank disk. Twice, thrice, she saw the
black arms move above the seething cauldron
in a strange fantastic dance.

Then, in a moment, as from a bolt, the body
was shot into the deep pool beyond the outer
fang-like rocks of the Linn.

Anabal Gilchrist turned, the foam on the
water not more wan than her white face.

With slow steps she regained the heathy
ground. She did not look back once, then, or
as she clomb the long slope to her home.

VII.

It was an hour before midnight when Oona awoke. So often had she slept in the woods, through the hot summer nights, that there was nothing strange or terrifying in the blackness of darkness about her. She could smell the pungent odor of the bracken, and, somewhere near, wild mint. The keen fragrance of the pines and firs everywhere prevailed.

Ah, she was in the forest: how warm and sweet it was! Where was Nial? Scarce more than this drifted through her mind; then the heaviness of sleep came upon her again.

The night waned. Dawn broke upon the eastern hills. Slowly the light travelled downward beyond the crests of the mountains. It reached the forest, and spread an unshimmering sheen over it, like the silver-calm on a green sea. Then, out of the sky a marvellous flower grew. It was a dusky rosy gray at first, as it lifted through the blue-black heaven, already steel-blue in the east. Green folds of pink un-

curled and fell languidly on each side, drooping
petals. There was a stir and quiver; then a
shaft of gold, another, and another. Suddenly
it was as though the heart of the flower burst.
In the yellow mist and radiance, wherefrom tall
waving foliage of golden fire moved, as though
fanned by a wind from within, a cloud of glowing flakes arose. These may have been the
wild bees that make the honey of Magh Mell,
or the birds of Angus Ogue, belovèd youth-
god of the yellow hair. Then the golden heart
of the miracle swelled, with a mighty suspiration. Petals of rose and gold-green and pale
pink, as of shells, unclosed from it. The vast
blue flower was aureoled now with an ascendant
glory.

One by one the stars melted into heaven.
Low in the southwest a planet seemed to divide,
'then to close again, in a nebulous gleaming
haze. Then this night-bloom slowly paled,
dwindled, and sank into a deep gulf. An indescribable fragrance, an almost inaudible rustling
sound, — faint, as the roar of the rushing world
is faint beyond all ears to hear, — filled the air.
The pulse of the world quickened. The green
earth sighed, and was awake.

Through her sleep Oona heard the croodling
of doves. Then a bleating fawn in a fern-covert
close by made her stir. Suddenly she half rose,

stared about her, and felt the breath of the
cool wind that, too, had been awakened by the
sun, and was now sighing softly through the
pine-glades.

Then in a moment there came upon her the
remembrance of what had happened.

With a cry she sprang to her feet. What of
her foster-father? Had he awaked in the gloaming and found the woman Anabal beside him?
Had he made peace, or was his anger even now
brooding terribly? Who had seen him home?
What would he say, what would Sorcha say?
Perhaps, even, he had fallen into the Linn, or,
it might be, he had tried to make his way home
alone through the forest, and now lay somewhere in its depths, blind and baffled?

Thus was the child wrought. But what could
she do, she wondered. Should she make her
way swiftly through the forest and up Wester
Iolair to Màm-Gorm, and there see if her foster-
father was in his bed and asleep? What would
he say and do? Once she had seen him in a
passionate rage, and her heart shook at the
remembrance. Perhaps he would kill her.
Does it hurt much to be killed, she wondered.
Then she thought of Nial. If she could find
him, he could discover for her that which she
feared to seek herself. Where would he be?
For nights past he had not been seen at Màm-

Gorm. He might be high upon the mountain, perhaps at Murdo's remote sheiling on Ben Iolair, by Sgòrr Glan. He might be at the cave Uav-an-teine, the great hollow cavern, dry even in winter weather, which lay but a short way above the Linn o' Mairg.

Yes, that was likeliest. Nial loved the place. There he might sleep, where no dew or rain could touch him, and with the sound of Mairg Water to be his lullaby through the dark. She would seek him there. But first she would go to the Linn, so that she might know that her foster-father no longer lay by the stream-side.

The heart of the birdeen lightened as she walked swiftly through the dewy fern. She began to call back to the cushats and other birds as they uttered their matin cries. Then she laughed, and broke into snatches of song.

The light was streaming down the strath as she emerged into the open glade above the Linn. Here, among the trees on the slope and in the many cavernous rocks and bosky hollows, deep shadows still lingered. It would be nigh upon an hour before the morning twilight waned hence.

A glance showed her that there was no one at the Linn. She ran down close to it, and peered eagerly here and there, on either side. There was no one visible. With a sigh of relief

she was about to step forward to take a sunrise
peep into the pool below the Linn, for the great
salmon she had never yet been able to descry,
when she stopped, because of the croaking of a
raven.

It was not lucky to go athwart the croaking
of a 'fee-ach' at sunrise. The great black bird
swung on an outspread bough of a hazel,
close to the Kelpie's Pool, and croaked with
harsh, monotonous reiteration. Oona stooped,
lifted a stone, and threw it at the raven, who
watched her closely.

"Fitheach! Fitheach! The way of the sun
to you! Be off, be off!"

Croak! Croak!

"Black fēe-ach, black fēe-ach, go where the
dead are, and do not cross my way, or I will
put a *rosad* upon thee!"

Croak! Croak! Croak!

Half angry, half glad, the child threw another stone; then turned, leapt from stone to
stone, till she gained the grass again, and then
went singing low towards the cave called the
Uav-an-teine.

The arch of it was still in shadow, and the
bracken on the brow of the arch: though the
rowan that leaned forward into the air bathed
its upper branches in sunlight. On the smooth
thyme-set sward beyond, the yellow shine lay, so

warm that the butterflies hovered in and out of the golden area.

With cautious steps Oona advanced. If Nial were there, she wished to surprise him while he slept.

She crawled to one side of the sun-swept cave, within which was still a warm dusk. Surely that was the sound of breathing? Yes; she could hear the steady rise and fall, faint though it was. With a smile she moved forward.

Suddenly she stood as one changed into stone. What was this? What did it mean? No sign of Nial was there. But, among dried bracken and dead leaves, blown or drifted there in autumnal days, and forming a place of rest fit for the weariest deer that ever leaped before the baying hounds, lay two figures, claspt in one another's arms.

For a moment the idea flashed across Oona's mind that the sleepers were Torcall and Anabal. Then she knew who they were, — for who had such a mass of lovely dark-brown hair as Sorcha, what man of the strath had the curly yellow hair of Alan? So that was where the lovers met! Once or twice, within these last few cloudless days and nights, she knew that Sorcha, when at length the restless lapwings had ceased their querulous crying in the moonlight, had slipt quietly from the house. She knew, too, that once at least Sorcha did not return till sunrise, for she had been awake, and had risen, and had seen her sister moving slow, through the dew, with so wonderful a look in her eyes, so beautiful, so strange, that she had not dared to speak, and had fled back to her bed, with a sob in her throat, she knew not why.

She smiled, and pondered how best to startle them. How she wished Nial were here also, so that he might laugh when Alan and Sorcha suddenly awoke and found themselves observed !

But, as she looked, the change that had already been at work in her of late, swayed her mood otherwise.

She rose to her feet, and leant against the green mossy boulder at the side of the cave. For a while she stood thus, her eyes intent upon the lovers. How beautiful Sorcha's face was, faint-flushed like that ! What a new strange light upon her face ! And Alan, — how tall and strong he was ! how bonnie the rippling gold hair of his head ! His fair face, whiter now than she had ever seen it, seemed cut out of stone, so sharp were the outlines. Thus, she thought, must Angus Ogue seem: Angus, the fairest youth of the world, whom none sees now, for he is of the Ancient People, who, though still among us, are invisible to mortal eyes. Often had Sorcha told her of him; sure, now, this was he?

Instinctively she looked to see if white birds hovered anywhere. For the olden tale said that the kisses of Angus Ogue became white birds, and that these flew abroad continually, to nest in lovers' hearts till the moment came when, on the meeting lips of love, their invisible wings should become kisses again.

No, there were no birds; none, at least, for her eyes to see.

The hot sunlight moved upon her bare feet. Soon it would reach her waist, she knew, if she stood brooding there; and when it did that, the glow would be upon the face of Alan, and he would awake.

A sudden fantasy took her. Almost she had laughed aloud. When she moved into the space opposite the cave, it was as though she waded in sunshine. Everywhere in the light the dew shone, filled with unburning fire.

She crossed the sun-space, to where a mass of honeysuckle drooped over a wild brier. With deft fingers she made a crown of this, starred with some pink wild roses, pluckt from a low bush beyond the brier; then, of the dusky yellow honeysuckle, wove a garland.

Decorated thus, and with sparkling eyes, she turned and faced the cave again. Soundlessly, she began to dance.

At first it was the mere joy of her laughing

glee. Soon, she hoped, Alan or Sorcha would
wake. Ah, then, how she would laugh, to see
them stare confusedly at her, dancing there in
the sunlight!

' But as she wavered to and fro in the sun-sea,
a dreamy pleasure moved her to half forgetfulness of where she was. A mavis on the
rowan over the cave began to sing, the strange
late song that sometimes wells forth in silent '
August, — at first, long, sweet, vibrant notes,
then a swift gurgling music, and then, as his
heart warmed against the sun, more and more
wildly sweet, till the hot air swung with the
intoxication of his rapture.

More and more, too, was Oona rapt as she
wavered to and fro. The swift rhythm of her
joyous dance wrought her as with a spell. A
dream lay in her eyes, now set far away, — far
away, where Angus Ogue was, and where the
sun rose, and the moon waxed and waned to
the singing of the White Merle.

The sunlight seemed to drift her onward, as
though she were a dancing wave on the forehead of the tide. Soon she was past the cave,
and still, as the sunbeams flickered, she leaped
and swayed, rapt in an ecstasy beyond thought
or heed.

Suddenly, the thrush ceased. There was a
whirr of wings; then a sharp, quickly repeated
strident cry.

9

Another second, and Oona was a laughing child again, crouched low in the bracken. Alan or Sorcha was awake, and had stirred!

Ah, no, she thought, she would not let them see her now. True, they might hear her, where she lay panting like a young bird escaped from a hawk. As soundlessly as she could, for her quick breathing and the rustle of the bracken, she half crawled, half ran, back the way she had come. Soon she was safe, for the pines enclosed her, and then the beeches and birks near the water-slope. From·behind a vast beech-bole she watched to see if she were pursued or seen. But no one came. All was as before; only, thé thrush did not venture back to the rowan, which now threw its flickering finger-like shadows on the smooth turf below in front of the cave.

VIII.

ALREADY the breath of the day was windlessly hot.

Flushed with her dancing in the sunlight, and with the languor of August in her blood, Oona listened eagerly to the cool sound of the running of Mairg Water.

The next moment she was free of her scanty raiment, and was by the stream-side. As she stood among a cluster of yellow irises, the sunlight lay upon the gold of her hair and the glowing ivory-white of her body, and then seemed to spill in yellow fire among the tall blooms about her feet. A faint green glimmer from the emerald iris-sheaths dusked the small white thighs.

A leap like a fawn, and she was in the water. A hundred miniature rainbows gleamed in the dazzle of spray as she splashed to and fro, after she had come to the surface some yards downstream. What joy it was to feel the cool brown water laving her body; to dive and swim like an otter; to float slowly with the current under overhanging foliage, and see the young sedge-warblers in the reeds or among the water-willows, or to look up at the curving boughs of a birch or rowan, deep green against the deep blue! Then the wonder and beauty to rest with outspread arms, and breast against the flow; to stare down into the mirroring depth, and see the flickering feathers of the quicken and the red rowan-berries marvellously real and near, with lovely shadow-birds flitting to and fro among the shadow-branches, and, strangest of all, another white Oona drifting like a phantom through that greenshine under-world.

When she swung round suddenly, and held herself back against the down-flow, as an otter half-alarmed will do, it was not because she was drifting too near the "race" just above the cataract. A strange sound came from the Linn, or beyond it. The noise of the water was in her ears, and she could not hear distinctly; but surely that noise was the cry of one in sorrow, and, at any rate, human.

With a swift movement she slid to the bank, caught at a tuft of flowering sedge, and then stood, dripping and all agleam in the sunlight, while with inclined head she listened intently.

Now she could hear more distinctly: certainly some one was by or near the Linn. The noise of the churned waters rose and fell in a long,

wavering, unequal sigh; and in one of the downward hushes her keen ears caught tones and
even words she fancied she recognized.

She hesitated for a moment as to whether to
run back for the handful of clothes she had left
upstream, but then bethought her that it was
only Nial and no stranger who might throw
stones at her as a kelpie — as some boys from
the strath, who at Beltane had been burning
small fires and cooking wild-bird's eggs, had
done many weeks agone at Nial.[1] How often
in her wanderings with Nial she had bathed, to
his wonder and awe at her white beauty, her
daring, her skill. As for him, though he loved
the running water almost with a passion, nothing would induce him to enter it, except when
alone and in the dim light. As a boy he had
been as much at home in it as any creature of
the river. But once, after he had come to know
Oona, and to find in her the one person in the

[1] In many parts of the Highlands it is still the wont of children at Beltane (May-day) to light fires in woods or on rocky
spurs, and there cook eggs, or play other pranks, sometimes
very fantastic ones. These meaningless observances are a
survival of the days of Druidic worship. Beltane means the
sacred fire. *Baal, beal,* or *bel* is not the actual Gaelic word for the
Sun, or the Sun-god : though the Druids may have had *Baal*
from the Phœnician mariners who came to Ireland. The ancient Celtic word is *bea'uil*, "the life of everything," "the source
of everything." *Beal* (pron. *bel*) and *teine*, "fire," give " Beltane " = the Festival of the Sun.

world whose soul did not loom too infinitely remote above his drear loneliness of spirit, he had leapt one dead-calm noon into the water; and there and then, for the first time, realized, in the phantom which swam with him or beneath him, the misshapen ugliness of his body, the savagery of his distorted head and features. From that day he had never entered the stream save at late dusk or on moonless nights.

So with swift steps, which left small pads of damp upon the rock-ledges, Oona ran towards the great boulder which overhung the cataract.

As she passed the place where, a few hours ago, she had left her foster-father and the woman Anabal, she glanced here and there for any trace of either she might not have seen be- fore. The next moment she caught sight of Nial.

She watched him curiously. What did it mean, she wondered. He was crouching, with his back to her, on the extreme of the ledge overlooking the kelpie's pool, — that deep cald- ron which received all that was at last disgorged from the maelstrom of the Linn. His head was bent forward, and sometimes he leaned on his hands, and sometimes swayed backward or side- ways.

What startled her more were the strange, wild, barbaric words that Nial was chanting, with thin, hoarse, monotonous wail. What was this rune he chanted? Why did he crouch there, chanting and swaying, swaying and chanting?

Sometimes he ceased for a few moments that crooning, mourning, appealing, inexplicable chant, and appeared to be speaking, and to gesticulate as he spoke.

Fantastic thoughts flashed through the child's brain. Perhaps it was the kelpie who was trying to lure Nial to her arms; or mayhap Nial had seen her,.and was putting a *rosad* upon her. She knew that the people of the strath, and even Murdo the shepherd — in truth, Alan, too, and perhaps Sorcha, though she would not say it — believed that the elf-man was in league with all the mysterious or dreadful creatures of the shadow, from the harmless " guidfolk" of the hill-hollow to the yellow-clad demon-woman who drove her herd of deer and sang her death-song, and to the dark and terrible kelpie who lurked in the deep pool in that wild place beyond the Linn o' Mair. Or, again, Nial might be uttering some incantation; or be at his old quest, the seeking of his lost soul.

Surely, it must be that, she thought, as soundlessly she approached him.

Within the last minute or two a change had come over him. Every now and then he raised his head, often clasping and unclasping his

hands, swaying to and fro the while, and speaking or chanting rapidly, with wild, scarce-coher-
ent words. He was as one in an ecstasy. Oona,
for the first time, feared him. She stood, only
a few yards behind him now, and listened.

"Ochan, ochone, arone! and so fair too, and so fair!
O white you are as the canna that floats in the breeze,
Or as the wool of the young lamb that Murdo found dead in
    the heather,
Or as the breast of Sorcha, or as Oona, little Oona!
O, O, arone, arone, Death of me, Woe!
Oh, white too and fair, and I black as the wet peats,
Black and ugly, so that even the deer know,
And Fior and Donn and all the dogs
Think me no more than a sheep, than the kye, ochan, ochone!
But oh, it 's dead you are and drowned, Anam, my Soul!
And it 's there you lie . . . gray and still . . . with . . .
. . . and you laugh at me, may be . . .
And it may be you are the shadow only that will go if I leap
    at you!
. . . and hair like mine thick with dew. . . .
Or . . . or the kelpie . . .
And true it was, with the fēē-ach, and the feannag, and the
    corbie,
The corbie, the hoodie-craw, and the raven!"

At these words Oona glanced swiftly to right
and left. Nowhere had she heard again the
croaking of the raven, and now she could descry neither of Nial's three birds of omen. But
just as her gaze was wandering back to the
dwarf, she caught sight of the *fitheach* further
down-stream, perched upon a dead branch near

some rocks, and even as she looked she heard
its harsh, savage *croak! croak!*

"*Ay, ay, ròc, Fēē-ach, ròc! Dean rocail, dean
rocail!*" began Nial again, with a wild
gesture. . . .

"*Nial! Nial!*"

He ceased all movement, all sound, as though
smitten into silence. Her fear partially overcome, now that she had gathered from his words
that he thought he had found his soul at last,
but that it was dead — yet with a dread in her
heart because of the *thing* that lay there in the
pool, whether alive, dead, or asleep, or treacher-
ously assuming life — she called again, and more
loudly, —

"Nial! Nial!"

Slowly he looked round. A bewildered terror
in his eyes waned. It was only Oona.

" Nial, Nial-mo-ghràidh, what is it ? "

" Hush, mo-mùirnean," he muttered, beckon-
ing to her to creep close to him. The slight
breeze that had sprung up for its brief life crept
along the stream, and whispered along the grass
and in the hot-smelling fern. The murmurous
sound of it made the child glance apprehen-
sively behind her. She dreaded the elfin foot-
steps that folk said could be heard at times near
Nial.

" What is it, dear Nial? "

" *Ssh !* Hush! Come here: look! . . . look! "
he whispered.

Gently she stole beside him, leaned over the
ledge, and stared down into the pool. A mere
breath of the breeze ruffled the surface, and all
she could see was a dark mass with a dusky-
white splatch, looming shadowily through the
amber water, and strangely distorted by the
silver shimmer caused by the wind eddy, which
came and went round the circuit of the pool
like a baffled bird.

" What is it? Who is it? What is it, Nial ? "

" Hush ! do not speak so loud. It is my soul."

" Your soul, Nial?"

" Ay, true. Sure it is my soul. All night I
was in the woods, and I heard a *tap-tapping*
going ever before me, and at dawn it led me
down by the Mairg, and then the spirit flew
away before me, and the *annir-choille* was just
like a woodpecker! And when it flew up by
the Linn I . . ."

" Whisper louder, Nial! I can't hear."

" When it flew up by the Linn I saw it change
into a curlew, and it wheeled over the Linn and
called *cian-cian-cianalas*, and then I was afraid,
though the annir-choille that was like a woodpecker had made hope to me of finding my soul."

" Who is the annir-choille, Nial? "

He gloomed at her silently. Then in a constrained voice, and with averted eyes —

"How should I know? I know nothing. I
am Nial."

"But what have you been told?"

"They call her the wood-maid — the tree-
maid."

"*Ah-h* . . . and Nial . . ."

"But when I came near, the curlew flew
away. Then it was that I looked into the pool.
And then, and then it was, Oona-mo-rùn, that I
saw my soul lying here — big as a man's soul
should be, and with a face as white as yours;
ay, a fair good body like Alan's, an' with clothes
on, too — dark, beautiful clothes; an' the hands
of him that moved about were white; an' . . .
oh, Oona-birdeen, look *you* now, and see if it is
not as I say!"

The awed child stared into the brown depths,
where the surface was still ruffled silvery here
and there, with a glinting, glancing shimmer
that made all things below shiftily uncertain.

"Do you see it, Oona?" cried an eager whisper at her ear.

"Ay, sure."

"Oona, Oona, is it dead? Oona, birdeen,
Oona-mo-ghràidh, it may — it *may* be living!
O Oona, the white soul o' me — white as you,
my fawn!"

The blue eyes glanced up from the pool,
and at the speaker. She looked at him, then
downward again.

" Nial ! "

" Yes . . . yes, Oona . . ."

" The wood-maid has been playing with you."

" No, no, no; that is not a true word on your lips ! "

" Sure, a true thing it is. Look, Nial; see how big it is. The white face of it is yonder by the salmon-hole, and one foot is moving against the rock below us ! "

" And what of that ! Sure, it is a beautiful soul, dead or alive; and big as a man's should be, and fair and white and strong ! "

" Nial . . . Nial . . . it may be alive, for I see its hands moving . . . but . . . but " — and here tears came into the child's eyes, and her voice shook with sorrow for her hapless friend — " but . . . Oh, Nial . . . so big a soul will never be able to creep into *your* body . . . for you are small, dear, small, and — and . . . an' then *it* is so big and strong ! "

Alas, the pity of it ! Never once had Nial thought of this; never had he dreamed that so large a soul could not get into his dwarfish, misshapen frame.

He stared in wild amaze, first at Oona, then at the drowned thing in the water — his soul, or a phantom, or a body, or mayhap the kelpie, he knew not which, now — then at Oona again. A fierce pain was in his eyes. He bit his lip,

in the way he did whenever Màm-Gorm struck
him, — a thing that had not been for months
past. A little rivulet of blood trickled into his
thin matted beard, tangled and twisted this way
and that like a goat's.

" Nial! Nial! " moaned Oona, pitifully.

" Ay, it is true . . . that is a true thing that
you will be saying, Oona. Sure, it would need
to be a soul as small as your own that would do
for poor Nial."

" No, no, Nial! " cried the child, comfortingly,
" bigger than mine, *really, really*, yes and . . .
and . . . fatter! "

A sob shook his heavy frame. Oh, the long
seeking, and the near goal, and the bitter futile
finding! Still, Oona's sympathy was sweet.
Dear birdeen that she was, to say he would
have a bigger soul than hers, bigger and fatter,
too. But no, he thought — no, better to have
one the same as Oona's, for all he was so much
older and bigger and stronger than she was.

" Ah, Oona-mùirnean, if I could only find my
soul at all — anywhere, anywhere! "

" But you *will* find it, Nial! You *will* find
it! Sorcha told me that you are *sure* to find
it. Never mind what they say down there in
the strath. What do *they* know about souls?
And . . . and . . . *Nial!* "

" Yes, my birdeen."

"If . . . if . . . you *can't* find your soul anywhere — and all this summer we 'll go seeking,
seeking, for it, till we have listened at every tree
in the forest and on the mountain side — if you
can't find it anywhere, *I am going to marry you!*"

Nial looked at the child bewildered. He
knew little of what marriage was, save that in
the strath two married people lived in one
house, and that the woman was called by the
name of her man, and that they were sadder,
and led duller lives, so at least it seemed to
him. Sure, it would be for pleasure that he and
Oona should have a cot of their own, though he,
and she too, for that, preferred the pinewood;
and a thing for laughter that she, the bit birdeen
Oona, should be called Bean Nial!

"Why would you be marrying poor Nial,
Oona my doo?"

"Because you would then have half my soul.
Yes, *yes*, Nial! don't shake your head like that;
I *know* you would. Sorcha told me it was in
the Book."

For the moment the outcast forgot what lay
in the pool. Of three things he stood ever in
awe. First, Torcall Cameron, the man of men.
Second, the Book, which was a mystery, and
held all the *sians* and *rosads*, all the spells and
incantations in the world, and, as he had heard,
was full of "living words," though never had he,

being soulless, seen any coming or going to it, like bees, where it lay on the shelf above Torcall's bed. Third, the inscrutable powers which worked somewhere, somehow, behind Torcall, before which even he, Màm-Gorm, was, almost incredible though it seemed, as mist before the wind.

When, therefore, he heard Oona speak of the Book, his awe held him for a moment spellbound. Never had he so much as dreamed that his name was even mentioned there at all. The wonder, the mystery of it, almost took his breath away. What an ill thing, then, that word of the preaching-man he had met once in the strath; who had told him, in answer to his asking, that he, Nial, could have no name in the Book of Life, because he was unbaptized, and a godless heathen, and a soulless elf-man at that! And now — now — Sorcha had seen his name in the Book— ay, and not in any poor small strath Bible, but in the great *Bioball* that was Torcall Cameron's own, up at Màm-Gorm,, on the hillside of Iolair!

But of that mystery he was to hear no more then and there. A cry had come from Oona, a cry of such terror, with moan upon moan, that his heart within him was as a flame in a windy place.

What had happened to the child? Was there

a spell upon her, he wondered; was *that* down there in truth no other than the treacherous, quiet-seeming, murderous kelpie!

He saw that she was shivering all over; that her body was as pallid as her white face.

Not a word came from her. She kneeled forward, staring stonily into the pool.

"Oona! Oona!" he whispered chokingly, terrified beyond further power of speech. Without averting her gaze, she slowly raised an arm and pointed at what had hitherto been but a blurred figure at the bottom of the water. The arm, the pointing hand, remained thus, as though paralyzed.

Nial bent over the ledge. The slight breeze had now passed. Not a breath shook the feather-leaf of a rowan. The sunflood poured out of the east upon the shimmering land. Though but an hour after sunrise, the heat palpitated. For the first time that morning there was no wind-eddy upon the pool. The brown water was as lucid as a mirror.

The thing — corpse, or soul, or kelpie — had begun to move. It was slowly rising to the surface.

He shuddered. This, then, was the cause of Oona's fear. Yet, even as this thought passed through his brain, he knew that there was some other reason for the frozen agony of the child.

The body ascended gradually, face downward, the arms trailing stiffly beneath it.   One
foot was still caught by the weeds, which had
caught it as in a net.   With a slow gyration
the corpse swung round, face upward.   The
weed-thrall gave way.   The drowned rose with
outstretched arms.

Oona shrieked, then sank back, cowering, and
covered her eyes with her hands. ' Nial! Nial
neither thought nor felt; he was stunned by a
blank bewildering amaze.   For what he saw, and
what Oona had seen, was the drowned body and
the dead face of . . . Tórcall Cameron!

In the awful, throbbing silence, broken only
by the turmoil of the Linn and by the incessant
moaning of the child, the dwarf stared as at
some horrible impossibility.

It *could* not be! ' Màm-Gorm, of all men in
the world!   Màm-Gorm, the great, strong, stern
man of the hills; no, no, no, sure, it could not
be!   Moreover, as he knew, Màm-Gorm never
left the hillside; in all the time he had known
him, he had never come nigh the Linn o' Mairg,
nor even near Mairg Water, and how could he
be there?   And would not Oona for sure have
seen him that very morning in his own bed
belike?   Besides . . . *Màm-Gorm* . . . it was
as though the preaching-man were to cry out,
" *There is no God!* "

At his ear he heard a moaning whisper: "*It is my doing ; it is my doing.*"

"Oona, Oona-lassie, is it mad that you will be?"

"O Nial, Nial, Nial! it is of me, this thing! Ay, sure, ay, sure! Oh, arone! arone! it was I who left him sleeping nigh the Linn last night, thinking to make peace between him and the woman Anabal that is Alan's mother! And oh, oh, she has gone away in the gloaming not seeing him, and he will be for going home when he wakes, and will be calling *Oona, Oona, Oona*, and I not be hearing him, for I was away in the wood, with the fear upon me! And then he will be moving through the dark, and — and — O Nial, *Nial!* He is drowned, drowned, and the water is on him because of *me!* Nial! Nial!"

The child swayed to and fro in her passionate grief. A new fear came upon Nial: that she might throw herself into the pool, to be drowned even as her foster-father was.

But at that moment both were hushed into staring silence.

Slowly the corpse began to sink again. Down, down, it went, leaning forward more and more, till it seemed as though it were standing upright on some unseen ledge of rock. Then, gradually, it revolved further, till once more it hung

suspended in the depths, face downward, and
with stiff arms adroop beneath.

Without further gyration, motionlessly it
seemed, the body sank, till it became blurred,
obscure, shapeless.   Then there was no more
of it than a black shadow far down in the brown
depths.

Oona rose to her full height. She gave a
long sigh, one short, choking sob. Her eyes
stared unwaveringly at nothing; the nails of
her fingers cut the small clenched hands. The
raven on the dead branch beyond the pool, that
had been croaking monotonously ever since she
had first heard it, became suddenly still.

Nial rose too.   He knew, without word from
her, without thought even, what she meant to do.

" Oona ! "

She did not glance round, but he saw her
throat quiver.

" My birdeen, my birdeen, ah, my bonnie wee
fawn !   Come back, come back !   Sure, it is not
him at all !   It is the kelpie, Oona, it is the
kelpie ! "   When the words came from her,
hushed and strange, he knew that she knew
the truth.

" I will be going . . . now."

" Oona ! come . . . " then in a flash his arms
were about her, as she leaped, and with an effort
that nearly hurled both into the pool, he swung
her back to the ledge.

There she lay on the grass-covered rock, white and still. Nial bent over her, moaning, trembling, moaning.

An hour later, Murdo the shepherd, coming down from the mountain, and going by the Linn o' Mairg, so as to reach Inverglas by the west side of the strath, heard a wild barking of his dogs. Through the heat-haze he stared indifferently, then curiously, at two stooping figures.

He approached the pool slowly. The dogs were silent. One had stopped, and was sniffing and staring, the other whined at his feet.

Yes, he was right, he muttered; it was Nial . . . and Oona! But what did it mean?

Both sat silently by the Kelpie's Pool. The wild, fantastic, shrunken figure of Nial was black against the light. He seemed as though rapt, spellbound. The child was naked, her shoulder reddening under the flame of the sun. He could see her strained, streaming eyes.

His heart beat quick with a vague fear as he moved towards them. He stopped, when Oona's low irregular sobbing was audible.

Beside him the collies crouched, whining.

Nial looked round, rose, and touched Oona. She, too, rose; her sobbing breath ceasing.

"Màm-Gorm is dead," said Nial, simply; "he is dead — *there*."

IX.

IN a brief space, Murdo learned what Nial could tell him. For all his shepherd-eyes, he could discern nothing in the pool but a vague blur of darkness far down.

What was he to do? He could not think, with these two staring at him there. Whispering to Nial that he would be back shortly, that he was going upstream to where Oona's clothes were, and adding that when he brought them back Nial was to lead the little lass away, take her home, find and tell Sorcha.

When, some minutes later, Murdo returned with the small bundle, he saw that the child was weary with heat and fatigue, as well as with what she had endured. There would be no trouble with her.

And indeed, when once she was in her scanty garb again, Oona went without a word. Nial whispered that he would be back as soon as he could; and would bring the gray horse with him.

The last Murdo saw of them was a momentary glimpse as they disappeared among the
bracken, under the pines.   The elf-man was
carrying the sleeping Oona in his strong crooked
arms.

The shepherd, who had betrayed no emotion
as yet, stood staring into the pool.   A mist
came into his eyes, and one or two tears rolled
down his furrowed face.   A grim satisfaction
moved into his mind, along with his dull pain;
for now he remembered how his father, who
had been shepherd on Màm-Gorm of Iolair
before him, had had " the sight" of this very
happening.   The old man had been laughed at
in the strath; though, by the waterside, he had
thrice seen Màm-Gorm's wraith rise out of the
Kelpie's Pool.   *Now* the foolish folk down there
would not be laughing.

After a time he bethought himself that Nial
might not be back for long.   It was nigh upon
noon, and he wished to get the body away as
soon as might be.   It was now he remembered
that Nial could not tell Sorcha, for he had met
her and Alan going after the kye to the hill-
pastures.   This was well, meanwhile.

At the Ford of Ardoch there was an old boat
not used for years past, save by himself, by
Sorcha, or by Alan.   In it were fishing poles,
a rope, and other things of his and Alan's.

They would serve now, he muttered. So once more the gaunt plaided shepherd strode up stream, mumbling as he went through his red tangled beard, and with his wild hill-eyes shining with the thoughts of life and death that were slowly filling his brain; thoughts, memories, superstitious fears, and vague, strange phantasma rising from the dull ache of sorrow.

To his ears, the most familiar of sounds, the bleating of ewes and lambs, came down from the mountain as a lamentable cry. That night there would be dread in his heart, because of the lonely hillside, and the wide darkness, and the wraith that would be moving through that darkness.

Soon he found what he wanted, and speedily returned. At first he thought he would need help, but after a time he decided to do what he could himself. To one of the long poles he fastened his shepherd staff, with its strong curved cromak.

The sweat poured from his face with heat and weariness long before he succeeded, at last, in getting a grip of the corpse. But, undaunted by failure after failure, and these even after he had first caught hold, he raised it slowly to the shelving ledge which ran out a few feet below the surface. The rest was easy. He slipped the rope over the feet, arms, and waist; then

slid the body along the slippery ledge, and so
with a rush to the face of the pool, and thence
to a wide cranny in the rock beside him.

Sure, there was no mistake. Màm-Gorm
himself, in truth; for all he was so quiet and
pale, with the dark frown out of his face now,
and all the stern, brooding life of the man no
more than an already nigh-forgotten idle song.

So this was the end of Torcall Cameron of
Màm-Gorm. There had been none prouder
and more aloof than he in all Strath Iolair.
Ay, he was a proud man. And now there was
an end of it all. Sure, it was a bitter ending.
God save us the dark hour of it. Ay, the dull
knock and the muffled voice that come soon or
late, in the mirk of day or night, at the soul-
gate of each of us — Torcall mhic Diarmid had
heard them. . . . Thus, over and over, variously, yet ever on the same lines, Murdo revolved in his mind the passing of Màm-Gorm.

At last, to his satisfaction, he heard the pecu-
liar cry which Nial was wont to give as a signal.
Then followed the trampling of a horse: finally
both appeared, coming along a stony path in
the forest that in winter was a clattering water-
course.

It did not take long for the two to lift the
body on to the small shaggy white horse, and
there to secure it; with the white face staring

blankly up at the blue sky, the open eyes
fronting with unwinking gaze the pitiless glare
of the sun. While they worked, Nial told
how he had carried Oona home, and laid her
on Sorcha's bed, sound asleep and warm. He
had feared to leave her there all alone, lest she
waked, or lest evil came to "her out of the
shadow;" but he did what he could, and that
was to take down the great Book from the shelf
by the bed where Torcall Cameron would sleep
never again, and lay it at the lassie's feet·
Then he had gone out to the kailyard, and let
Donn the collie leave her two pups awhile, and
had given her a shawl of Sorcha's to smell, and
then had sent her up the mountain to seek for
Màm-Gorm's daughter, wherever she might be
with the sheep and kye.

As soon as all was ready, the crossing of the
Mairg Water was done at the Ford, and then
the ascent begun to Ardoch-beag. Murdo
stalked in front, the rope-bridle looped over
his arm. Raoilt, the white mare, staggered
and stumbled after him up the craggy path.
Then came Nial, his shape not more fantastic
than the shadow which waxed and waned mockingly before him, as he toiled upward, with
bent head and tear-wet quivering face.
Finally, lagging some yards behind, limped
Murdo's two collies.

The August heat-wave silenced every bird on the hillside. Not even the grouse cluttered. Far away, in a marshy place, there was a drumming of snipe.

The air was heavy with the smell of honey-ooze from the pale ling and the purple bell-heather. Now and again there was the sharp twang in it of the bog-myrtle, sweltering in the sun-glow. ʼ

The thin dust rose from the path, or even from the face of the granite rocks. The shadows of the wayfarers lay pale-blue against the hill-road, when the path widened into it. The dogs crawled, panting, their long tongues lolling like quivering bloody snakes. Nial wearily wagged his shaggy peaked head to and fro: at times, too, he let his great swollen tongue fall half out of his mouth, as though to cool the thirst of it against the parched air. Poor Raoilt sweated at every pore of her body, while dark streaks of wet ran down her flanks. Murdo showed less fatigue; but his weather-brown face had become deep red, and about his moist brow a haze of midges hovered. Quiet and cool, one only: cool and quiet, the rider on the white horse, for all that his face was as baked clay in the yellow glare, that his staring eyes were upon the whirling disk of flame in the zenith.

With a sigh of relief Murdo saw at last the cottage of the Gilchrists, sole house on the easter side of Tornideon.

Not a word had he said hitherto to Nial as to the taking of the corpse to Ardoch-beag. If the dwarf had thought of a destination at all, apart from Màm-Gorm, it was doubtless of the minister's house, which lay three miles beyond Ardoch-beag, at the far end of Inverglas.

But suddenly he waked to the knowledge that Murdo was off the road, and on the path leading to the byres of the widow Anabal.

What was the meaning of it, he asked; but Murdo would not hear. As they stopped at the ring-stone, between the byre and the cottage, he went up to the shepherd.

"Why will you be doing this thing, Murdo MacMurdo?" he demanded.

At first the man gloomed upon him, then he smiled grimly.

"Wait."

Having said this, Murdo strode to the doorway of the cot. He knocked; there was no answer. He knocked again; again no answer. Then he opened the door. He did not expect to see Alan, but he was sure the woman Anabal would be in. There was no trace of her. The bed had not been slept in. The peats were black in the fireplace. Yet, strange to say, an open Bible lay on the low deal table, and on the near page was a pair of horn spectacles.

It was very strange. Well, he would search everywhere, both but and ben, outhouses, and byre, and stable.

There was not even a dog about the place.

He returned to Nial, downcast.

"There is a spell upon this place, Nial-of-the-Woods. I wish we had not come."

"Why did you come?"

"This, man, this — *this* — is why!" he muttered savagely, and as he spoke he drew from his pocket a gold ring.

"That is one reason, Nial-of-the-Woods! Look you, I found that ring in a crevice in the rocks on the further left side of the Linn o' Mairg. Look you again, I know the ring. Do you see these letters? Ah, well, you can't read, poor elfin-creature that you are; but I'll tell them to you. They are *F. G.* and *A. G.* And now will you be knowing what *F. G.* and *A. G.* are for? They are for Fergus Gilchrist and Anabal Gilchrist — *and this ring here, that I found by the Linn o' Mairg, is the wedding-ring of Anabal Gilchrist!*"

The outcast stared, vaguely impressed, but without understanding what Murdo was driving at. The man saw he was puzzled, so with a rough gesture he pulled him over to the near

flank of the mare. "And here, you poor fool
— *to Himself be the praise, for this and that!* —
is the other reason. Look at *that!*"

What he pointed to was a long tress of gray
hair, gray-streaked brown hair, firmly clutched
in the right hand of the dead man.

A glimmering of Murdo's meaning came into
Nial's mind. He glanced at the shepherd,
appalled.

"Ay," whispered the latter, divining his
thought: "sure that there is nothing else but a
tress of the hair of the woman Anabal. And
you be telling me, Nial, if you can, what
Anabal Gilchrist was doing last night or to-
day afore dawn, that she should leave her
golden wedding-ring lying by the Linn-side,
and that a tress of her hair — and there is none
like it, no, none o' that witchy gray-brown, in
all the strath — should be held even now in the
death-grip o' Torcall Cameron o' Màm-Gorm?"

"And that is why you have come here,
with . . . with . . . *him?*"

"That is why."

The two looked at each other. A fierce
anger and lust of revenge burned in the heart
of the shepherd. To Nial everything was
simply a horrible incomprehensible mystery.
But Murdo knew something, perhaps more than
any one else, of what had lain between Torcall

Cameron and Anabal Gilchrist; whatever the
outcast knew, or vaguely surmised, was too
deep down in his mind now to swim up into
remembrance.

It was Nial who broke the silence.

"What of Alan?"

"The curse is upon him too — to the Stones
be it said!"

"He will be far up on the north side of
Tornideon . . . or with Sorcha on Iolair."

"The woman must have fled. Or . . . ah,
for sure that thought was never coming to me.
Nial, my man, you never thought o' that, did
you? You never thought that perhaps there
were *two* bodies down there in the pool! Ay,
for sure, for sure: Màm-Gorm was not the
man to die alone!"

"Perhaps . . . Murdo, perhaps it was . . .
perhaps it was . . . *he* who . . ."

The words failed. The gaunt shepherd
looked down at the speaker, frowning darkly.

"May be, may be," he muttered at last. "If
I thought *that*, I would be letting him lie in
his own house. Nial, see that no word o' this
gets upon your lips if you meet any one. No
one must think *that*. No one in the strath
must think an evil thing o' Màm-Gorm."

Once more Murdo left, and made a diligent
search everywhere. When he came back, he

was muttering constantly, with a wild look
in his eyes.

"Did you hear *that?*" he asked in a hoarse
whisper.

"That? What? I heard nothing."

"Did ye not hear some one in the shadow
ayont the byre crying, *Cian! Cian! Cianalas!
Dubhachas!*"[1]

"No, no," murmured Nial, trembling; "I
saw the shadow of a bird on the grassy place
yonder, and a cry like the *binn fheadag.*"

"Ay, the feadag, the feadag, but no flying
bird, for 't was a wraith playing the dark song
of the dead on the shadowy feadag that no man
has ever seen, though there be those who hear
it . . . God save us!"

Nial shuddered. It might be so, he thought.
He believed he had seen a plover only, had
heard no more than the wailing cry of a
plover; but doubtless Murdo *knew.*

The shepherd stood staring at him gloomily.
At last he spoke.

[1] Pron. *Kī-ăn! Kī- an! Keen-ăl-ŭs! Doov-ăch-ŭs!* To
Celtic ears, not unlike the wailing cry of the plover. The
words, moreover, mean " For long, ever ! Melancholy ! Gloom !"
The word *feadag* (pron. *Fădd'ăk*), in the ensuing sentences,
has two meanings, — a plover, and a flute. The *binn fheadag* is
" the shrill voice of the plover." Murdo turns the word both
ways : *feadag,* the bird, and *feadag,* a flute ; the flute made of
wind and shadow that sometimes is heard on the hills when a
(*tamhasq*) *tăvăsk* moves through the gloom of night.

"This is a dark thing, Nial, my man.
There is no light upon it to me whatever.
But it will be looking to me as though I should
go down to the pool again, and be seeing if *she*
is there too.   And if not, then I must seek out
Alan upon the hill.   Do you think this thing
too?"

Nial shook his head despondently; he could
think neither one way nor another.   Màm-
Gorm lay there dead — white, stiff, staring up
to the sun.   He knew *that*.

"Ah, poor fool that you are," Murdo went
on, pityingly, and as though talking to himself; "sure, I need not be asking you.   How
can a soulless thing o' the woods think: wi' a
head like an addled egg, and a poor bit body
withouten a spirit in it, as all decent folk have.
Well, well, 't is Himself has the good reason,
praise be His!   And, now, Nial, I will be
doing this thing.   I told you the Book lay
open on the table in there.   Well, I will be for
going by whatever the word is that is on my
sight when I first look.   If it tell me to go into
Inverglas, and speak of this evil day, then it
is going there I will be; if it tell me to go and
seek in the pool, well, I will be going there;
and whatever I see, it will be the way for me.
If I am to speak, it is speaking I will be; if I
am to be silent, it is silent I will be."

And with that the shepherd turned, moved slowly away, and entered the cottage for the third time.

Where would he look, he wondered, when he stood by the table, and stared down upon the open Gaelic Bible. Sure, he would accept the sign in the sentence across which Anabal's spectacles lay.

He stooped, and with pointing finger read slowly and with difficulty, word by word:—

"Cuir, a Thighearna, faire air mo bheul; gléidh dorus mo bhilean!"
"Set, O Lord, a watch before my mouth, keep the door of my lips!"

"That will be enough," he muttered with bated breath, and went out. As he approached the horse, Nial saw that he had found the "wisdom." Vaguely he wondered if Murdo had noticed any "living words,"—mysterious phrase that ever perplexed, and sometimes terrified him.

"Nial, I have found the word. It is not for me to go into the strath with news of the dead. The Book said, 'Keep a watch before the mouth, keep the door of the lips.' You understand . . .? Ay, sure: poor faithful creature that loved Màm-Gorm; ay, an' that Màm-Gorm, too, loved as much as Donn or Fior or

any o' the dogs, wise beasties. . . . Well, '
I will be go'ing now, down to the pool: then,
one way or the other, I will be looking for
Alan Gilchrist. An' it is for you to wait here,
Nial, lest he or any other come. We'll put
the mare and . . . and . . . Màm-Gorm . . .
into the byre just now. And you wait, you
will be minding!"

In silence Raoilt, with her rigid burden, was
led into the hot gloom of the byre. Then the
door was partially closed, for there was no fas-
tening to it, and Murdo made ready to go.

"Leave me one o' the dogs," said Nial,
sullenly.

"And for why?"

"I will not be staying here alone, in this
treeless, foreign place, Murdo MacMurdo; no,
that I won't, unless you will be leaving me one
of the dogs."

The shepherd grunted surlily, for the collies
were his best friends, and good company. But
if so to be, then so to be. He would take
Braon and leave Luath. It was safer, at such
a time, to be alone with a dog, than a bitch:
for bitches were known often to be in league
with demons and evil spirits. As for Nial,
not being human himself, there would be less
risk. Now that he noticed it, there was a red
glare in Luath's eyes, and the bitch moved

about in a strange way. For sure he would take Braon.

The time went wearily for the watcher at Ardoch-beag. The sweltering heat made him long doubly for the green forest that was his home. He did not dare enter that lonely house. Who or what might be sitting there, or standing looking at him from the inner room? Neither could he venture into the byre, though, but for her awful burden, he would rather have the company of the mare Raoilt than of the bitch Luath.

For a long while he sat in the shadow of a dyke that was the south side of the winter sheepfold. But he grew more and more uneasy as time passed. What if Murdo did not come back till after nightfall?

He rose and stared about him. Where was Luath? He could not see the collie anywhere. He had noticed her trotting idly up the steep bend of the road beyond the cottage.

" Ah, there she is," he muttered, as he saw a shadow flit bluely across the blinding way. But what was the matter with the beast? She came along at a swift, slinking run, her tail skiffing the ground between her feet. As she passed, she gave him a furtive glance. The upper lip, taut, just showed a glimmer of white fangs.

" Luath ! Luath ! Luath ! "

But the collie would pay no heed; or, rather, she paid this heed, that she broke into a race, and flew down the road to the Ford till she was no more than a black blur beyond a whirling eddy of dust.

This was the last straw. Nial gave one look more all around him. Then he listened at the byre, to hear if Raoilt were munching at her hay. What if Màm-Gorm should get tired of being dead, and should dismount, and, rigid and white, step out into the sunlight? The thought made him shiver, for all the blazing heat.

Silently as his shadow, he was out upon the road. Suddenly the whim took him to go the other way rather than by the path he and the others had come. Below Cnoc-Ruadh the road dipped for a bit; and there was a sheep-path from it that would lead him down to the ford of Ath-na-chaorach, whence he would soon be in Iolair forest again.

But no Ford of the Sheep did Nial see that day.

For after he had reached the summit of the road at that part, to the westward of Ardoch-beag, he saw a sight that brought the heart suffocatingly to his mouth. It was this, then, that had made Luath slink swiftly away, with curled lip and bristling fell.

There, as though carven in stone, sat the
woman Anabal, rigid and motionless as the
thing that was in the byre. She was on the
extreme verge of Cnoc-Ruadh, where a double
ledge runs out from the great boulder which
overhangs the strath, and whence for nigh
upon a score of miles the eye can follow the
course of Mairg Water.

At the far end a heat-haze obscured moun-
tain-flank, and bracken-slope, and birk-shaw,
all save the extreme summits of the hills,
purple-gray shadows against the gleaming sky.
Nearer, in the north strath, the smoke of many
cots, sheilings, and bothan rose in their perpen-
dicular or spiral columns of pale blue mist.

From where Nial stood he could see her face.
It was as wan and awful as that of the dead
man in the byre, but he saw that the eyes lived.
The woman sat dumb, blind, oblivious of the
flaming heat, her gaze fixed, unwavering. Fire
burned in them, a fire that would never be
quenched, till the day of the grave.

He could not tell whether she was alive or
dead, whether a woman or a wraith. But he
noted the long tangled locks of hair which
hung over her shoulder, brown hair streaked.
with gray, like the tress that the dead man still
clutched in his right hand.

It was a thing to flee from. One desire only

possessed him now, to reach the safe green quietudes of the pine-forest once more. There all was familiar; there he could evade man or wraith.

And so he, too, left that solitude, where, once again, Torcall and Anabal were nigh one to another, and not knowing it.

How could he know: none but God knew: that in the woman's ears was the roar of the Linn for ever, that the laughter of a kelpie wrought her ever to an excruciating terror. Dumb, motionless, staring unwaveringly: so was she at the flame-red setting, as she had been since the first blaze had lightened along the peaks of the east.

X.

IT was within an hour of nightfall when, from the verge of the forest below Màm-Gorm, Nial caught sight of the kye coming down from the hill-pastures. He could not see Sorcha, but he knew she must be there; probably with Alan, who for days past had been wont to depute his own shepherding on Tornideon to a herd-laddie who lived with an old drover just beyond the Pass of the Eagles.

Nial had already been up at the farm. Oona lay where he had left her, and was still in the same profound and, but for her low breathing, deathlike slumber. Thence he had wandered back to the forest, thinking that he would descend towards the Linn o' Mairg, and see if Murdo were still there in his quest for Anabal. He had scarce entered the pine-glades when, happening to glance backward, he saw the cows coming home.

Sure enough, in a few minutes Sorcha appeared: and, as he had surmised, Alan with

her. They walked together, his arm about her
waist, while slowly they followed the leisurely
kye. As they came nearer, Nial heard Sorcha
singing one of her many milking songs. Often
he had heard her sing that which now came
rippling down the heather, and he could have
given her word for word for it.

    "O sweet St. Bride of the
        Yellow, yellow hair:
    Paul said, and Peter said,
    And all the saints alive or dead
    Vowed she had the sweetest head,
    Bonnie, sweet St. Bride of the
        Yellow, yellow hair.

    "White may my milking be,
        White as thee:
    Thy face is white, thy neck is white,
    Thy hands are white, thy feet are white,
    For thy sweet soul is shining bright, —
        Oh, dear to me,
        Oh, dear to see,
        St. Bridget white !

    "Yellow may my butter be,
        Soft and round ;
    Thy breasts are sweet,
    Soft, round, and sweet
    So may my butter be :
    So may my butter be, O
        Bridget sweet!

    "Safe thy way is, safe, O
        Safe, St. Bride:
    May my kye come home at even,
    None be fallin', none be leavin',

Dusky even, breath-sweet even
Here, as there, where O
   St. Bride thou

" Keepest tryst with God in heav'n,
   Seest the angels bow
And souls be shriven —
Here, as there, 't is breath-sweet even,
   Far and wide —
Singeth thy little maid
Safe in thy shade,
   Bridget, Bride ! "

Nial hesitated. He would have gone to her
at once, but he did not wish to speak before
Alan. Moreover, what was he to say to Angus
Ogue, as Anabal's son was called by the strath-
folk on account of his beauty and because he
was a dreamer and a poet, though but a shepherd of the hills. How could he tell of Murdo's
quest by the pool, and also of the spirit or
wraith he had seen sitting on Cnoc-Ruadh that
is beyond Ardoch-beag on Tornideon?

The flanks of the cows gleamed in the light
as with filled udders they swung slowly homeward, their breaths showing in whorls of mist
whenever they were in shadow, where the dews
were already falling after the extreme of heat.
Behind them, now on a sloping buttress of rock
and heather, now on the smooth thymy hollows
which lay like green pools among the purple
ling, Alan and Sorcha moved, both bathed in

the sunglow, his left hand clasping her right
and swinging slow. Ah, fair to see, thought
Nial: fair to see.

But, even while he pondered, he saw Alan
take Sorcha in his arms, kiss her, and then
with lingering hand-clasp, turn to go up the
mountain again, or, as might be, to cross to
Tornideon. Not far did he go, though: for, as
Nial watched, he saw Sorcha's lover lean against
a great boulder, where he stood like a fair god,
because of the sunflood falling upon him in gold
waves out of the west. Beautiful the rolling of
that sea of light, across the sloping surface of
the forest: with the yellow-shining billows flowing and rippling among the summits of the
pines, and ever and again spilling into branchy
crevices or dark, green under-glooms.

Doubtless Alan was waiting to see her reach
Màm-Gorm, and perhaps for a signal thereafter:
if so, thought Nial, he had best see Sorcha at
once, though he knew not the way of the thing
to be said, or if he could speak at all while
Oona slept.

Slowly he moved towards her. She had
descried him, for she did not follow the cows,
but stood, waiting. The gloaming was already
about her. She was like a spirit, he thought,
with the windy hair about her face — for with
the going of the sun a sudden eddy had arisen,

and the air of its furtive, wavering pinions was upon Sorcha.

"Nial!" she cried blithely, when he was a brief way off: "Is the peat-smoke a bird that it has flown away from the house — for not a breath of smoke do I see? Is father in: and Oona? Have you seen her? I've called thrice, but St. Bridget herself would n't be having an answer from Oona if she's hiding somewhere. *Oona . . . Oona . . . Oona !*"

"Don't be calling upon the child, Sorcha. She is tired, and is sleeping."

"And father?"

Then in his heart of hearts Nial knew that he had not the courage to say what he had to say. Sure, too, there was something he did not understand. After all, the woman he had seen on Cnoc-Ruadh, could be no other than Anabal Gilchrist. And if *she* could be drowned, and yet come alive again, perhaps Torcall Cameron could, ay, was perhaps already up and, blind as he was, feeling blankly round the walls of the strange place he was in, to be out soon, and, later, in the dark, come striding into Màm-Gorm.

"And father, Nial, and father? Is he in, or is he out upon the hill, with the gloom upon him this night again?"

"It will be a strange thing that I am telling

you, *Sorcha-nighean-Thorcall*, but one that will
be glad and warm in your heart."

" Speak."

" There is . . . there is peace now between
Màm-Gorm and the woman Anabal, that is
mother of Alan."

" Peace! oh, Nial! To Himself the praise of
it! Oh, glad I am at the good thing that you
say. Sure, glad am I ! "

" It is true. Ay, and he has gone over to
Tornideon, and will sleep this night at Ardoch-
beag."

Sorcha stared bewildered. Even her joy at
the news, which meant so much for her' and
Alan, was forgotten in sheer amaze. Her father
go to Tornideon, her father asleep at Ardoch-
beag!

Words of his came to her remembrance: she,
too, muttered "my soul swims in mist."

" Nial, is this — a true thing?" . . .

" Ay."

" Is it — is it — a true thing that he is up at
Ardoch-beag, and will sleep there . . . and . . .
and . . . is at peace?"

" Ay, sure, he is up at Ardoch-beag, and will
sleep there, and sure, too, sure he is at peace."

A wonderful light came into the girl's beautiful eyes. Her twilight beauty was now as a
starry dusk.

"Nial," she whispered, " dear Nial, you and
Murdo see to the milking of the kye for me
this night . . . do, dear good Nial, do! And
you can ask Oona, too, to help you . . . for
. . . for, Nial, all is well now . . . and I can
go to Alan . . . oh glad am I, and like as
though a bird sang in my heart! "

And then, before he realized what he had
brought upon himself, before he could say a
word of yea or nay, Sorcha had turned, and
with swift steps was hurrying through the
gloaming to where Alan still stood on the hillside, watching and dreaming, dreaming and
hoping.

Nial stood gazing after her. Strange this
mystery of beauty. All his trouble waned out
of the glare of day into a cool twilight. The
passing of her there on the hill was like music
in his ears. Ah, to be Alan, to have so tall and
strong a body, so fair a face, to have Sorcha's
love, to have a soul! The fairer soul the fairer
body; that seemed to him a truth — for what
had he to go by but the three he knew best
and loved best, Oona and Sorcha and Alan,
the fairest man, the most beautiful woman, the ·
loveliest child he had ever seen or dreamed of
there in Strath Iolair, or during those mysterious wanderings of his when he was far from
the mountain-land with the gypsy-people. No

beauty like theirs, no others like them in any
way; sure, it was because the souls of them
were white, and all three kindred of the forgotten "people of the sun," whom Sorcha sometimes sang or spoke of as the Tuatha-de-Dánan,
and Màm-Gorm had told him once were old
forgotten gods — fair, deathless folk.

In truth it was with joy that Sorcha hastened
towards Alan. He saw the light in her eyes
before she was near enough to speak. Often,
beholding her, he was aware of something within him that was as a sun-dazzle to the eye that
looks upon a shining sea or a cloudless noon.
Sometimes his heart beat low, and an awe
made a hushed, fragrant, green-gloom dusk in
his brain; sometimes .he grew faint, strangely
wrought, as a worshipper when the spirit for a
brief moment unveils its sanctuary and irradi-
ates, transforms the whole trembling body, but
most the face and the eyes of wonder. At
other times all the poet in him arose. Then
he laughed low with joy because of her beauty;
and saw in her the loveliness of the mountain-
land. Then it was that she was his " Dream,"
his " Twilight," his " Shining star," his " Soft
breath of dusk." Dear she was to him as the
fawn to the hind, sweet as the bell-heather to
the wild bee, lovely and sweet and dear beyond
all words to say, all thought to image. Then

there were their blithe hours of youth — hours
when he was *Alan-aluinn* and she *Sorcha-
maiseach;* seasons of laughing happiness, and
light ripple of the waters of peace.   Children
of the sun they were in truth, in a deeper sense
than they, as all the kindred of the Gael, were
children of the mist.

But of late both — and he particularly — had
been wrought more and more by the passion of
love.   Ever since the refusal of the minister at
Inverglas to marry them, because of the feud
between Torcall Cameron and Anabal Gilchrist,
and of the ban laid by each against the offspring
of the other, they had troubled themselves no
more about what, after all, to them, in their
remote life in these mountain solitudes, meant
little.   In the dewy, moth-haunted, fragrant
nights of May, when it was never quite dark
upon the hills, and even in the forest the pine-
boles loomed shadowy, they had become dearer
than ever to each other.   Day by day thereafter
their joy had grown, like a flower moving ever
to the sun; and as it grew, the roots deepened,
and the tendrils met and intertwined round the
two hearts, till at last they were drawn together
and became one, as two moving rays of light
will converge into one beam, or the song of two
singers blend and become as the song of one.
As the weeks passed, the wonder of the dream

became at times a brooding passion, at times
almost an ecstasy. Ossian and the poets of old
speak of a strange frenzy that came upon the
brave; and, sure, there is a *mircath*[1] in love now
and again in the world, in the green, remote
places at least. Aodh the islander, and Ian-bàn
of the hills, and other dreamer-poets know of
it — the *mirdhei*, the passion that is deeper
than passion, the dream that is beyond the
dreamer, the ecstasy that is the rapture of the
soul, with the body nigh forgot.

This *mirdhei* was now more and more upon
Alan; upon Sorcha, too, the dream-spell lay.

So it was in a glad silence that he watched
her coming. For the moment she was not
Sorcha, but a *Bándia-nan-slèibhtcan*, a goddess
of the hills, fair as the *Banrigh-nan-Aillsean*,
the fairy queen. Often, singing or telling her
some of the songs of Oisìn mhic Fhionn, he
had called her *his* Darthula, after that fairest of
women in the days of old, because she too had
deep eyes of beauty and wonder. Therefore
the word came out of his heart, like the single

---

[1] The " mircath," or war-frenzy, is *mire-chath*, the "passion of
battle," as the "mirdeeay" is *mire-dheidh*, the "passion
of longing." The word Darthula — *infra* — is a later Gaelic
variant of *Dearduil* (almost identically pronounced), the Sco-
to-Gaelic equivalent of the Ersc *Deirdrê*, the most beautiful
woman of old.

mating-note of a mavis, when, as she drew nigh to him and whispered low, "*Alan! Alan!*" he murmured only "*Darthula . . . Darthula-mo-chrce!*"

In a few words she told him the marvellous news: Torcall and Anabal at peace; her father now at Ardoch-beag!

At first he too could scarce believe it. Then, little by little, the smaller wonder waned, and the wonder of his love — the wonder of Sorcha grew.

Hand in hand they wandered slowly up the mountain as in a dream. A strange new joy had come to them. The world fell further away, far beneath them. Even the strath became a shadowy place — a foreign strand where their voyaging boats need never coast.

When the moon rose, first through a tremulous flood of amber-yellow light, thence to emerge as a pale-gold flower, low in the *Lios-nan-speur*, the "garden of the starry heavens," the mountain lovers were already far up Ben Iolair, and nigh the great Sgòrr-Glan, the precipice that on the eastern flank falls sheer from the Druim-nan-Damh, the Ridge of the Stags, for close upon two thousand feet. Here in a sheltered place known as the *Bad-a-sgailich ann choire-na-gaoithe*, "the shading clump of trees in the windy corrie," was the sheiling of Murdo the shepherd, which for weeks past had been used by Alan rather than his own hill-sheiling high on Tornideon, where the east wind blew with a fierce breath, and the hill-slope was barren, and there was no Sorcha.

They could hear the wind among the heights, but the moon-wave was everywhere with quiet light, and there was peace.

For a while they stood at the door of the cot. The moonshine touched them with a beam of pale gold — a finger out of heaven. Silent and still it was: no sound but the furtive crying of the wind among the invisible corries and peaks, with a flute-like call among the serrated pinnacles of the Ridge of the Stags. At intervals, as a vagrant breath, came the sigh of the hill-torrents as they fell towards the Srùantsrhà, the wild stream that foams from the lochan of Mairg beyond the Pass of the Eagles, and surges hoarse and dark, even in the summer droughts, at the base of the great precipice of Sgòrr-Glan.

Hand in hand they stood, silence between them. Their eyes dreamed into the moonlit dusk. In the mind of Alan Sorcha moved as a vision; in the mind of Sorcha there were two shadowy figures of dream — Alan, and the child over whose faint breath of life in her womb her heart yearned as a brooding dove.

When Oona awoke she saw that it was dark.
In the peat-glow she could descry the figure of
Nial crouching in the shadow of the ingle, his
gaze fixed upon her.

"What is it, Nial; what have you been
doing?"

The dwarf saw that as yet she had not remembered. He feared for the child, though he
knew not, what none knew, how the strange
fatalism of the race was already strong within
her, strong and compelling as hunger, thirst,
or sleep.

"Oona, my fawn, you must have food. I am
hungry too. You have not eaten since last
night."

A startled look came into her eyes. He saw
it, and hurriedly resumed —

"So, a little ago, I lit the peats, which had
smouldered into ash; and now, bonnie wee
doo, I will be making the porridge for you,
and see . . . the water is boiling that is in
the kettle, and I'm thinking it is singing
*Oona, Oona, mochree, Oona, Oona, mochree,
come and be having the food with poor Nial!*
And, Oona, look you, there is the warm milk,
and the bread; for I milked the brown cow
Aillsha-bàn, when Sorcha went up the hill
with Alan. An' I couldn't be milking the
white one, Gealcas, for she wouldn't give

without Sorcha's singing, an' I could not be
minding that song; no, not I; but I knew the
song for Aillsha-bàn:—

> "Aillsha-bàn, Aillsha-bàn
> Give way to the milking!
> The holy St. Bridget
> Is milking, milking
> This self-same even
> The white kye in heaven —
> Ay sure, my eyes scan
> The green place she is in,
> Aillsha-bàn, Aillsha-bàn:
> And her hand is so soft
> And her crooning is sweet
> As my milking is soft
> Upon thee, Aillsha-bàn —
> As my crooning is sweet
> Upon thee, Aillsha-bàn,
> Aillsha-bàn —
> So soft is my hand and
> My crooning so sweet,
> Aillsha-bàn!"

Poor Nial's singing was not restful, for his
voice was at all times shrill and hoarse, and
now it had an added quaver in it.   But Oona
listened, drowsily content.

She had remembered all.   Yes: Sorcha was
right that day when she said Death roamed
through every hour, and that the moment
before each new hour Death stood at the door
and broke the link that held the going and the
coming in one bond.

If her foster-father was dead, he was dead. The fact was absolute to her. Once she had seen a stag die. She had been up near the summit of Iolair, and was about to quench her thirst from a small black tarn, hid among the rocks, when she caught sight of a wounded deer. The hunter had maimed, not slain it: and though it had escaped, it was only to sink with weariness by the tarn, and lie there watching its blood trickle steadily into the crimsoned water, till there should be no more flow. As long as life remained in the stricken beast, Oona could not believe in the possibility of death. In its extremity it made no further effort when she drew close; only a gurgling sob showed its broken heart, and great tears fell from its violet eyes. Either instinct let the stag know that she would do it no harm, or it was too weak to resent a touch; but in the end the dying deer let Oona take its nozzle in her lap, while she smoothed the velvety skin and wiped away the blood and sweat. Even when kissing it and calling it tender impossible names, she saw the veil come over the eyes, she could not admit that death could come *then — there.* But when there was not a quiver, and the rigid limbs were cold, her tears dried, and she looked at it meditatively. It was dead; what had she in common with it?

A little ago, her heart throbbed with loving
pity; now she glanced at the great beast curiously.   Its strong odor was disagreeable; its
bloodied mouth and breast disgusted her.
There was no good in being sorry.   It was
dead.

In a different, but kindred way, her foster-
father was the stricken deer.   She had seen
him almost to his death; she had seen the
drowned body; almost she had died of her wild
and passionate grief.   Then she had slept
through the noon-heats, and the afternoon, and
the evening: and now she awoke to the no
longer overwhelming but irrefutable fact, that
her foster-father was dead.

She had meant well.   Why did the woman
Anabal not see to the blind man?   But it did
not matter.   He was dead now: dead.   God
willed it so.   It was to be.   Not all the striving in the world could have prevented this.   In
wild winter nights, before the peats, she had
heard Torcall himself chant the rune of Aodh
the poet, with that haunting ending which
Sorcha sang often to herself; that Alan had
on his lips at times as always in his heart;
and that even Murdo muttered when it was
tempestuous weather, and Death was abroad,
and the gloom of the rocks was heavy upon
him.   Ah, the words evaded her; but Nial

would know, Nial, who was the tuneless harp
that caught all wandering strains, from sheil-
ing-song to the way of the wind among leaves.
"Nial, what is the thing that Sorcha sings
often . . . and that . . . that *he* sang sometimes, about the quiet at the end?"

Nial stared, puzzled for a moment; then he
repeated in a low voice —

"Deireadh gach comuinn, sgaoileadh :
Deireadh gach cogaidh, sìth ! "

Over and over Oona murmured the words:
"*The end of all meeting, parting: the end of all
striving, peace.*"

She was tired. She would think no more
about her foster-father. He had seen God by
now. He would know why she ran away from
the Linn: and how the fear was upon her in
the wood; and, afterwards, how the sorrow of
him pulled at her heart. And now . . .

How she wished Sorcha were home, to sing
to her. Warm was the peat-glow, and she was
tired. She closed her eyes again, murmuring
drowsily the refrain of an old song.

Silence was in the dusky room again. Nial
sat crouching by the fire: patient, as was his
wont. There was not a sound within, save
the low breathing of the child and the dull
spurtle of the flame among the red fibres on

the undersides of the peats. Outside there was a melancholy wail in the sough of the hill-wind.

The first hour of the dark passed. What was the night to bring forth, he wondered. Where was Murdo? What had he found?

Another hour passed. A weary sleep was on him. He dozed, woke, stared at the shadowy figure of Oona, dozed again. At last he too slumbered, the *duain-samhach* that is too calm for dreams, too deep for sorrow.

It was in the middle of the third hour that he stirred because of the howling of a dog.

Nial could do what was impossible even for Murdo the shepherd: he could tell in the dark, and by the sound only, which of the dogs barked. He knew now that the howling came neither from Donn nor Luath. It was not the coming of Murdo then, for these were his two dogs, and that was not the howl of either. If they were near, their baying would be audible.

Yes, it was Fior. She must have left her pups, and be roaming round the sheiling. Why was she not in the barn? What had alarmed her?

If it were not because of Oona, he would go and quiet her. Tenderly he glanced towards the bed. He rose slowly, his heart beating.

In the flicker of the fire he saw the child,

sitting upright, her eyes wide open and staring
fixedly.   .

She said no word. He feared to speak.
Her unwavering gaze disconcerted him, though
now he saw that it was not upon him. He
would just whisper to her, he thought:

"Oona-mùirnean, Oona-uanachan, it is only
Fior. She will be baying against the moon,
because of the spell against her pups."

She paid no attention to him. He shivered
as he saw that her eyes were now unnaturally
bright: and that their gaze shifted, as though
they followed one who moved about the
room.

The child shivered, but seemed more in
startled amaze than dread. There was more
fear in Nial than with her, when he heard her
speak.

"Why do you come here?"

Nial stared. There was no one visible.

"*Is coma leam thu!* I hate you, I hate you!"
cried the child, with a passionate sob. "Go
back to him. I left him with you! He is not
here; he is dead . . . he is dead . . . he is
dead!"

Trembling, the dwarf advanced a step or
two.

"Oona! Oona! It is I, Nial! Speak to
me!"

"Stand back, Nial: The woman Anabal, wife of Fergus, is speaking to me."

With a groan he staggered to one side. Was she here, then, and not still sitting on the great rock overlooking the strath? Sure, then, a spirit must she be: and no wraith now, for his eyes were void of her.

But for all his dread, he must guard his lamb. If only he knew one of the spells in the Book, that he had placed at Oona's feet!

"And what will An — what will she be saying to you, my bird?"

"She says: *Leanabh, dh' èirich dha; dh' èirich domh; eiridh dhuit!*"

Nial slowly repeated the words below his breath: "*Child, it has happened to him; it has happened to me; it will happen to you.*" Oona must be ill, he thought; as Murdo was two winters ago, that time he came back from the strath, on the last night of the year, lurching and swaying, and saying wild meaningless things.

"And what else will she be saying to you, birdeen?"

"*Thig thu gu h'anamoch!*"

"*Thou shalt come later;* sure now, dear, there is no meaning in that! Oona, my bonnie, lie down; lie down, wee lassie, and sleep, and sleep!"

But even as he spoke, he saw a change in her face. It was like moonshine suddenly moving on dark water.

He caught fragmentary words . . . *suain . . . sìth . . .* and then, with "sleep" and "peace" still on .her lips, she lay back, smiling.

Slowly and soundlessly he approached the bed. In the intense stillness he heard his breath going like the slow, heavy beat of a heron's wing. Outside, the baying of the dog had suddenly ceased.

She was asleep, or nigh so. He stooped, and kissed the yellow tangles that overspread the pillow.

Her lips moved.

What was the thing she whispered? He could not hear; ah, she was murmuring it again . . . *anail . . . breath of . . . breath of a . . .*

"*Hush-sh-sh,* birdeen," he whispered low; then, seeing that her lips again muttered drowsily, he put his ear to them.

"*And then . . . she . . smiled . . . and said: Do not . . . fear!* (a pause, a sigh) *. . . sacred is the . . . breath . . . the breath of . . . a mother.*"

The child slept. He stole back to the ingle. There was peace now; even the wind, though

it moaned and swelled more and more loudly,
was as a soothing song.

And so the night passed; Nial sleeping
fitfully, waking often, and ever when he woke
pondering that last saying of the child, "Is
blàth anail na mathár."

XI.

THAT night, any wayfarer going down Strath Iolair, between the Pass of the Eagles and Inverglas, must have been startled by a windy blaze of flame against the slope of Tornideon.

Since sundown the wind had increased in strength. The loud clarion-call could be heard unceasing on the hills. Through the pass it came with long wail or dreary sough, then with a howl would swoop along Mairg Water, with a noise that washed away the roar of the Linn.

One man, at least, saw it. Under an arch of rock, in a space half filled with fragrant dry bracken, Murdo the shepherd watched.

Doggedness was at once Murdo's strength and weakness. He had been convinced that Anabal Gilchrist, guilty or innocent, had perished along with Torcall Cameron. He had come to the Linn, and till he found her he would wait. Moreover, had he not the word of the Scriptures for it, bidding him be silent? What need, then, for him to go about as an idle rumor? - All would be known in time, without *his* telling.

When at last the twilight came, he was still
there. If he could not see the body of Anabal
in Mairg Water — and he knew that, if there, it
would soon or late be swirled out of the Linn
or the Kelpie's Pool — he would wait till he saw
her wraith.

There were many things — like certain stories
told of the speed of great vessels at sea, and
about what the electricity, out of which the
lightning came, could be made to do — which
he doubted, or at least discounted in the telling.
But in the sure wisdom of his fathers, he knew
there was no rock of stumbling; therefore he
was well aware that the wraith of the dead
comes to and fro between its death-place and
that darkness which is deeper than the mirk of
the blackest night, on the night following its
severance from the body. So, he would wait
and see. If her wraith came from up the strath
or from down the hill, he would know that she
had not died in the water. Wherever it came
from, he would follow it.

He had seen too much, he muttered again
and again to himself, with quaking heart: he
had seen too much in hill-gloamings and drear
mountain nights to have fear of the wraith of a
poor widow-body, who lived no further away
than over against Cnoc-Ruadh on Tornideon.
The moaning and loud soughing of the wind

tried him sore. But the night was cloudless, and the moon hung above Iolair, a beacon everywhere in the dark. Then, too, as the hours went, he grew warm and comfortable in his rocky lair; moreover, fresh text after text came into his mind. In multiplicity of these was safety; even were some of them no more than "And Chelub, the brother of Shunah, begat Mehir," or than that (to Murdo, blasphe- mously familiar) saying in Isaiah, "In that day shall the Lord shave with a razor that is hired," —though, sure, to his shepherd mind, there was comfortable word as of home, as well as sacred influence, in "And it shall come to pass in that day, that a man shall nourish a young cow, and two sheep."

He had been dozing when the first spurt of flame broke out upon Tornideon. A little later he roused with a start, and looked out upon the pool. There was a gleam there, or somewhere;, could it be the woman Anabal?

Then his gaze was drawn swift and steadfast, as iron to a magnet. He realized what and where the flames were. Ardoch-beag was on fire.

In a moment there flashed upon him the recollection of Màm-Gorm, on the white mare Kaoilt, in the byre there.

With the thought came another, that he had

been mad to believe Anabal was in the pool at
all. She must have discovered the body of
Torcall, and set fire to the place — corpse, mare,
and byre! There was not a moment to lose.
Yet; perhaps it was Alan; well, even then, he
muttered, he must go. But supposing . . .
but supposing . . . that . . . that Màm-Gorm
himself . . .

Murdo did not know what to do. The dogs
would help him, he thought. Crawling from his
hiding-place, he whistled to Donn and Luath.
Both collies had already crept from the fern,
and were standing, with stiffened tails and rigid
bodies, intently watching the shooting, darting,
leaping, ever-spreading flame on the hill opposite. Abruptly, Luath began to growl. Then
Donn stole, whining, to the shepherd's feet.

"What ails the dogs?" he muttered, half
angrily.

A few minutes later his keen eyes discerned
the cause of their uneasiness. The full flood of
the moonlight was upon the flank of Tornideon,
and it was now possible to see along the whole
path from Ardoch-beag to the ford, *glan mar a
ghrian*, as he said to himself — clear as in the
sunlight.

And this was the thing that Murdo the shepherd saw, to be with him to his death-day, and
to be forever in Strath Iolair a legend of terror.

Down the steep descent that began to fall
away a few yards beyond Ardoch-beag, he saw
a tall, gaunt woman, with rent garments and
long, loosened hair fluttering in the wind, striding down the hill-way, often with wild gestures.
And before the woman trampled and snorted a
horse, mad with the fear of the flame, and knowing, too, it may be, the awful burden of death
it bore, now swung cross-wise, upon its back.
As a mad horse will do, it pranced in a strange,
stiff, fantastic way: wild to leap forward and
race like the wind from what lay behind, from
what jerked and jolted above; yet constrained
as by another than human force.

Ever and again, in a momentary lull of the
wind, Murdo could hear its shrill, appalling
neighing. Once, too, he shrank, because of the
screaming laughter of the woman.

Furlong by furlong he watched this ghastly
march of the dead and dying. Were it not for
the flames at Ardoch-beag, where both house
and byre were now caught in a swirling blaze,
he would have believed the other to be no more
than a vision.

With difficulty he silenced the dogs. He
would stay where he was now, and see what
was going to be done that night: for it was
clear that Anabal, seemingly mad, and having
set fire to Ardoch-beag, was now driving Raoilt

and its corpse-burden either down to Mairg Water, or with intent to cross and go up the mountain of Màm-Gorm.

This last, indeed, was evidently her aim: for, when at last the ford was reached, Murdo could see her striving to make the affrighted mare enter the shallows. Raoilt, however, would not budge. With fore-legs planted firmly, with head thrown up, quivering flanks, and long tail slashing this way and that, the white mare showed some strange horror of the swift-running ford-water. Suddenly she swung round, and with a grotesque prancing moved along the north bank towards the Linn.

They were now close to him. Murdo could see the bloodshot, gleaming eyeballs of Raoilt: the white, set face and staring eyes of Anabal. Either the roar of the whirlpool, or the sight of one of the collies slinking terrified through the fern, added a new terror to the mare. She swerved wildly. The burden she bore became still further unloosed. With scraping hoofs she pawed at a bank of heather, in a vain attempt to find solid footing. A · plunge . . . a fall backward . . . a staggering recovery among the very rocks of the Linn . . . and . . . freedom at last!

But, for the second time since Murdo had last seen him in life, Torcall Cameron was hurled headlong into the Linn o' Mairg.

With a cry, the shepherd sprang forward.
Anabal heard, but did not see. All she knew
was the roar of the Linn, the wail of the kelpie,
and *that*—that withering scream of the dead man.

For a moment she stood on the verge of the
cataract. Her arms were upraised: her whole
body moved with one unutterable supplication:

" *Fergus! Fergus!* "

The wild appeal rang through the night, above
the turmoil of the falling water, the increasing
moan and loud blasting vehemence of the wind.

Murdo did not see her leap or fall. His gaze
had for a moment sought the mare, who, at
that cry, had leaped as though stung by fire,
and was careering at break-neck speed up the
boulder-strewn bank by which she had come.

But when the shepherd looked again, Anabal
Gilchrist was gone.

Throughout that night there was a wilder
sound on the hillside than any wail of the wind.
This was the screaming of the white horse, as,
wrought now to a death-madness, it leapt way-
wardly through the dark, so passing from height
to height upward along the whole mountainal
flanks of Iolair.

At dawn, in the sheiling high up on Druim-
nan-Damh, Sorcha awoke, trembling.

For a time she listened in awe to the majesty

of the wind, a vast choric chant that filled the morning-twilight with an ocean of flowing sound. Then, again and again, she heard that strange, horrible scream.

Alan stirred. She whispered, as she drew closer to him. He, too, listened. A great fear lay upon both. This screaming voice in the night was an omen of sorrow, of doom. Who could it be but the Bandruidh — that evil sorceress of the hills, dark daughter of the Haughty Father, who had already won the soul out of Nial?

Sleep was impossible. It was banished even from thought, when a wild neighing close to the walls of the cot made Sorcha cry out, and cling to Alan as though death were already upon them.

They lay shuddering. Clearly this was one of the water-bulls or water-horses which roam the mountain-ways on nights of storm: dread demon-creatures, to see whom even is almost certain death.

"It will not be long till sunrise," Alan whispered; and by that Sorcha was comforted, for she knew that the ravening thing outside would have to haste back to loch or river or sea.

And by daybreak, in truth, the beast was already away. They heard the clamor of its hoofs against the granite stones and rock, as it sped upward still.

When, hand clasping hand, they ventured to
go out, they could see no living thing but an
eagle soaring high above the extreme peak of
Iolair: for the light of the new glorious day
was in their eyes as they faced the Ridge of
the Stags.

But suddenly Sorcha caught sight of something white leaping against the sunrise.

Alan's gaze followed her trembling arm and
outstretched finger.   He, too, saw, but unrecog-
nizingly, a white horse, prancing and screaming along the verge of the granite precipice of
Sgòrr-Glan.

The mad beast was now on the Sgòrr itself.
Behind were deep corries and ravines: in front,
nothing but the flaming disk of fire, nothing
but that sheer blank wall of granite, straight
from the brow of the Sgòrr to where the Srúan-
tsrhú surged darkly its tortuous way, two thousand feet below.

A faint impalpable mist was in the air.
This, doubtless, it was that made the white
horse loom larger and larger, till it stood out
against the morning, vast as Liath-Macha, the
untamable phantom steed "gray to whiteness,"
that Cuculain the Hero rode triumphantly
through the valley of the shadow of death.

Then it was as though it leaped against the
sun itself.

XII.

WEEK after week went by, changelessly fine, so that in the strath men began to shake their heads ominously because of the long drought. In the memory of none had there been an autumn so lovely.   For a brief spell, in mid August, coming indeed with the storm of wind which had helped the flames utterly to consume the few poor buildings of Anabal Gilchrist on Tornideon, great clouds had travelled inland from the Atlantic, and had burst floodingly upon hill and valley.   But in less than a week the sky was clear again, and of a richer, deeper blue.   The whole mountain-land was veiled in beauty.

The woods at the end of October were, other than the pine forests, a blaze of glory.   Few leaves had fallen, except from the limes and sycamores, and these sparsely only . . . scarce enough to lay a pathway of flakes of yellow gold before the hinds and fawns that trooped through the sun-lit glades.   The innumerable rowan-trees wore fiery hues upon their feathery foliage: everywhere the scarlet berries suspended in blood-red clusters against the blue sky or the cool greenness.

The dream, the spell, was not only upon the beautiful green earth. It lay elsewhere than there, or in the deeps of heaven: elsewhere than on the quiet waters, which slept against the shores beyond the mountains, and slumbered immeasurably towards the ever-receding west, with a soft moaning only, wonderful and sweet to hear.

For it was upon the heart and in the brain of each of the mountaineers of Iolair: but most upon Sorcha and Alan.

For them the days had gone past, days of rapt happiness in that golden weather. Already the world had become to them no more than a dream. They went to and fro, hushed, upon the hills, each oblivious of all save the other, all save the ceaseless thrilling wonder of the pageant of the hours from dawn to moonset. That strange rapture which comes at times to isolated visionary dreamers upon the hills, wrought a spell upon Alan. Scarce less was it upon Sorcha, and that less only, if at all, because of the second life that she sustained. The "mirdeeay" was a glamour in their eyes, in their mind, in their heart, from the hour of the

waning star to the coming of night. Not all
an evil thing is it to dream. The world well
lost! Ah, shadowy-eyed dreamers that know
the secret wisdom, it is well to dream.

None of the strath-folk saw them now. The
people murmured against them, because of the
tragic mystery of the deaths of Torcall Cameron
and Anabal Gilchrist. Little had been learned
from Murdo, and none now encountered Oona
or Nial. But a dropt word, a reluctant admis-
sion, a careful evasion, from the shepherd,
went far. Hints grew into a legend: soon a
perverted yet not wholly misleading version
of the facts became current.

On the same morning when, from the moun-
tain-sheiling, they had seen the white mare,
screaming in her madness, leap from the precipice of Sgòrr-Glan, as though full against the
sun, Alan and Sorcha learned from Murdo what
had happened. Below all the grief and horror
of the double tragedy, there was one thing not
to be gainsaid. The hand of God was here.

After their first passionate sorrow they whispered this thing the one to the other. It was
ordained. God had wrought thus with the
threads of all their lives. There was none to
blame, neither Torcall nor Anabal, nor the
child Oona, unwitting instrument of the divine
will. *Is duilich cuir an aghaidh dàn:* who

can oppose Fate, who set himself against Destiny?

A strange thing, that had a terrifying signifi-
cance for the strath-dwellers, was this: never were the bodies of Torcall Cameron and Anabal Gilchrist found. The Linn was dragged, the Kelpie's Pool poled over and over, the lower reaches of Mairg Water were examined under every shelving bank, or wherever a sunken bole or submerged boulder might have caught the castaways. No trace was seen anywhere, then or later. Possibly it was true, what an old man of Inverglas averred: that there was a slope at the bottom of the Kelpie's Pool, which ran in beneath a shelving ledge, whence the water poured down a funnel-like passage into a cavern filled with stalactites, through the innumerable holes and crannies at the base of which the flow vanished even as it came.

He had this knowledge, he said, from his father before him, who in the great drought of the first year of the century had seen the pool shrunken so that a man might stand in it and yet not be wet above the knees. "And the word of my father will not be for doubting," the old crofter added: "for he lived with God before him till he died, and now was with his own folk in Flaitheanas itself, praising Himself for evermore."

Thereafter, as was but natural, the home upon Tornideon being no more, Alan and Sorcha lived at Màm-Gorm. There was none to dispute their possession, for Torcall Cameron was without blood-kin, and all that was his was Sorcha's.

So week after week went by. Even in the strath the people said: " It was willed." There was no man or woman among them, even of those who were angry with Sorcha that she was not wedded before the minister — forgetful, always, that it was the minister who had refused to wed Alan and Sorcha, because of the feud between Torcall and Anabal (and, though none had inkling of it, because of the sin he knew of that lay between them, the sin that lived and moved and had its being in the person of the child Oona), and still more who were angry with her because she came never among them, but was as one lost to the world, and she too with the second life in her, when she ought to be seeing and talking to older women-folk — there was none among these who, in his or her heart of hearts, did not recognize that it is ever an idle thing for small wings to baffle against a great wind. *It was to be: it would be.* That was the unspoken refrain of all thoughts: the undertone of all comments.

The tragic end of Anabal Gilchrist, the doom that had fulfilled itself for Torcall Cameron: what was either but apiece with the passing of the ancient language, though none wished it to go; with the exile of the sons, though they would fain live and die where their fathers wooed their mothers; with the coming of strangers, and strange ways, and a new bewildering death-cold spirit, that had no respect for the green graves, and jeered at ancient things and the wisdom of old — strangers whom none had sought, none wished, and whose coming meant the going of even the few hill-folk who prospered in the *màchar*, the fertile meadows and pastures along the mountain-bases? *It was to be : it would be.*

Among the old there was exceeding bitterness. An angry and a brooding pain frowned in many hearts. But, alas, what good to meet the inevitable with wailing? What had to be, surely would be. Old wifeless men, old childless women took comfort in that bitter-sweet saying of the Psalmist: "Is iad lobairtean Dhé spiorad briste," — "*The sacrifice of God is a broken spirit.*"

But, with the harvesting, the strath-folk forgot for a while the very existence of the mountain lovers.

Smitten with the strange rapt elation of their

dream, Alan and Sorcha still went to and fro as though spell-bound. Sometimes he herded the cows alone: as before, Sorcha milked the sweet-breath kine, singing low her songs of holy St. Bridget or old-world cadences rare and nigh-forgotten now as the *Fonnsheèn*, the fairy melodies once wont to be heard on the hills and in remote places. But, though apart for a brief while, it was only to dream the more.

Yet, strange to say, Alan knew in his heart that this could not endure. It could not be, for overlong: God, soon or late, lays winter upon the heart, as well as upon the song of the bird, the bloom of the flower.

Nevertheless, he had no trouble because of this. There is, at times, in deep happiness, a gloom as of dark water filled with sunlight. While the glow is there, a living joy, the gloom is no more than the quiet sorrow of the world.

Often, of late, he had noticed upon the hillside, upon brier and bramble, fern-covert or dwarf-elder, that indescribable shadow of light, visible too at full noon in that golden weather as well as at the passing of the sun: that glow of omen, known of Celtic poets and seers in far-gone days. The first line of a fragmentary rune, come down from one of these singers who walked nearer to nature than does any now among the sons of men, was upon his lips over and over, because of this thing:

"Tha bruaillean air aghaidh nan tom."
"There is boding gloom on the face of the bushes." '

Once only the gloom lay upon him, the gloom that is upon the mind as a dark cloud upon a field of grain. What if ill should have come to Sorcha?

He turned, and went swiftly home. The gloaming had fallen, and Sorcha was sitting before the flaming peats, with claspt hands and dreaming eyes. She was crooning, half breathing half crooning a song, low and sweet against his ear as the noise of a running brook heard in sleep as one fares by green pastures under a moon strange and new in a strange land. And the song was one he had not known, not since he was a child, and heard Morag, the wife of Kenneth, foster-brother of Fergus Gilchrist, sing it before, in a day of mourning, she brought forth her first-born:

"An' O, an' O, St. Bride's sweet song 't is I am hearing, dearie,
Dearie, dearie, dearie, my wee white babe that's weary,
Weary, weary, weary, with this my womb sae weary,
And Bride's sweet song ye hear it too, and stir and sigh, my
    dearie!

    "Oh, Oh, leánaban-mo,
    Wee hands that give me pain and woe:
    Pain and woe, but be it so,

'T is his dear self that now doth grow,
Leánaban-mo, leánaban-mo,
'T is his dear self one day you 'll know
Leánaban-mo, leánaban-mo !

" St. Bridget dear, the cradle show,
My baby comes, and I must go,
Leánaban-mo, leánaban-mo !
Arone ! . . . Arò !
Arone ! . . . Arò !"

He had stood in the shadow, silent, listening with awe and a strange joy. His heart yearned to go to her, but he knew that a mother's first tears were in the dreaming eyes, and that it was not for him, or any save God, to be seeing them.

So Alan turned, and went up through the dusk to the low green summit of Cnoc-na-shee, a brief way from the sheiling. And when he was there he looked and saw nothing in all the light-gloom sky but one star low in the south — *Reul-na-dhuil*, the star of hope. Peace was in his heart. He kneeled down and made a prayer for Sorcha, and the child she bore, and for him, too. And when he rose, and went home, and looked back at green Cnoc-na-shee, he saw there for a moment a figure as of an angel, shining bright.

Night and day they were alone there. Murdo the shepherd was up at the high sheiling on Ben Iolair, and rarely came to Màm-

Gorm save to help with the kye, or do what
was needed about the steading. Oona, too,
was seldom seen of them; and of late, even
she had not always come at sunrise for the
food Sorcha placed for her on the bench by
the door each morning. As for Nial, he was
for long seen of none, save Oona, and where
and when that was no one knew.

As October waned, the day of the mountain
lovers became more and more a life of joy.
Hand in hand they would sit on the bench in
the sun, happily content: or dream, hand
clasping hand, before the glowing peats. It
was in vain that Murdo, fearing "the quiet
madness," reproached Alan, urging upon him
that he should go down into Inverglas and see
to the sale of the cattle and the sheep. The
young man shook his head, smiled gently at
the shepherd, and once at least murmured
those ominous words: "There is a time for
all things, and it is my time to be still. I
have peace."

Sorcha, being heavy with child, could not
now walk far, and indeed cared little to go
beyond the door-bench, or, at farthest, to the
green slope of the hillock of Cnoc-na-shee.
Her beauty had not waned, because of her
trouble. Her eyes had grown more large and
beautiful: wonderful stars of light to Alan

always — stars that shone out of infinite depths, wherein his soul could sink till it reached that ninth wave of darkness which is the sea of light beating upon the coasts of heaven.

.So, ever and again, glad with his joy and ungrievingly gloomed because of the shadow that day by day wove a closer veil about his spirit, he not grieving because not in himself knowing the mystery, he went out upon the hill-side, or into the forest. Often it was, then, that he heard the singing of Oona in the woods at sunrise and during the hot noons. Sometimes now, too, when late-wandering through the forest at gloaming, he saw afar off the still figure of Nial crouching by the tarn, or seated with bent head among the flags and rushes of the drought-dried pools. More than once, as he went home by the remoter glades, he heard the elf-man chanting wildly among the pines at night.

It was on one such evening that, returning with his mind strangely troubled because of the soulless man of the woods, and of his futile quest and the bitter wrong and pity of it, he was met by Murdo, with startling news. Sorcha had had a vision; and, being wrought by it, had fallen into premature labor. But she was not alone. He, Murdo, had brought his foster-sister, Anna MacAnndra, back with him from the clachan by the Ford of the Sheep: for as he had gone down with some young ewes that noontide he had seen a look like death in Sorcha's face, so white and drawn was it with sudden pain. Anna, he added, was a leal friend and dear to Sorcha, so that all was well.

And that night, in truth, the child of their great love was born to them. A night it was of pain and joy, of agony and rapture. But when at last the long-waited dawn came — when, as the woman Anna said, there was no more need to fear, for the death-hour of woman in travail was well past — there was deep breathing of quiet happiness upon the sleeping mother, deep slumber of birth-weariness upon the child that lay against her breast, deep peace in the heart of Alan.

It was not till the eve of that day that Sorcha told him of her vision. She had been sitting in the sun upon Cnoc-na-shee, when she was amazed to see three people pass from the forest and make their way up the hill. Because of the noon-glare she could not discern who they were, though each seemed vaguely familiar. Dark in the glowing light, their figures were visible, till they reached the ancient stones beside the cairn of Marsail. There she thought they passed into the long hollow beyond; but, when she looked again, she saw that they were now four in number, and that they were coming down the kye-path to Màm-Gorm. Her heart had begun to waver; but it was not till they were half-way down that she recognized the white faces of them: Torcall her father and Marsail her mother, Anabal and her man Fergus. All four walked in peace. And she heard a thin song in the air, that may have been from them, or may have been behind her, — a song that said, "*Beannachd do t'anam is buaidh*, — Blessing to thy soul, and victory," "Blessing, blessing to thy soul, and peace!" But still the spirit in her was strong, for why should she fear, dead, those whom she had loved, living?

But as they drew nearer she saw the woman Anabal waving her arms slowly as she advanced, even as the prophesying women of old did before the Lord; and, so waving, she chanted a rune. And the rune that she chanted was the *Rune of the Passion of the Mother* that no man has ever heard since Time was, and that has been in the ears of those women, only, who are to lose life in the giving of a life unto Life. So, hearing this rune, she fell sobbing, with the pains already upon her: and but for the coming of Murdo with Anna she would have borne her child on Cnoc-na-shee, the fairy hill — and who

knows but its doom might have been that of
Nial the soulless?

This vision, Sorcha added, she would not
have told to any one had she felt the death-
breath enter her as the child was delivered;
but now that the boy was born, and was so fair
and lusty, blue-eyed and golden-haired as his
father had been before him when he too was a
breast-babe, and, too, that all was well with her,
she told it. Moreover, sure no harm could
come of a song of peace: and as for the Rune
of the Passion of Mary, it was no more than an
idle tale that saying of Anna MacAnndra's and
of other women, that whoso shall hear it shall
surely die within the birth-month.

And because of her smiling lips and loving
eyes, and of the fair lusty child whose little
hands wandered clingingly about the white
breast of Sorcha, Alan believed that the ancient
wisdom was an idle tale.

When the dark fell, and pine-logs were thrown
upon the red-hot peats, the two talked in low
hushed tones, with eyes that ever sought each
other lovingly, dreamed and talked, whispered
and dreamed, far into the night.

Then, with close-clasping arm holding her
child to her bosom, as though in her exceeding
weakness — a weakness nigh unto death, now
that it seemed to float up to her from within,

rather than descend upon her from above — she feared her white blossom of love might be taken from her, Sorcha sank suddenly into drowning sleep.

Sitting by the bedside, with his hand stroking or holding hers, Alan revolved other thoughts than those of love only.

Passing strange, passing strange, this mystery of motherhood over which he brooded obscurely. And, truly, who can know the long, bitter travail of the spirit, as well as the pangs of the body, which many women endure — except just such a woman, suffering in just that way? Can any man know? Hardly can it be so. For though a man can understand the agony of birthtide, and even the long ache and strain of the double life, can he comprehend the baffled sense of overmastering weakness, the vague informulate cry against all powers that be?—Man, overlord of the womb: God, overlord of men. How many women have prayed, not to Him, but to the one Pontiff before whom all thoughts bow down, worshipping in dread : to that shadowy Lord of the veiled face, whom some call Death, that Woman of the compassionate eyes whom others call Oblivion, because of the poppied draught she gives the weary to drink, and the quiet glooms of rest that she holds in the hollow of her hand, and the husht breath of her that is Forgetfulness.

Thoughts such as these, though in crude words and simple symbols, were in Alan's mind.

No, he knew: never again could he even listen to men jeering at birth. He, though he had come to her virginal-pure, yet feared Sorcha's eyes at times, because — though not knowing it for what it was — of the deep-buried spiritual anathema which, in the gaze of the purest and noblest of women, affronts the chained brute that is in the man.

Ah, do men know, do men know — many a woman cries in her heart — do men know that a woman with child dies daily: that she wakes up to die, and that she lies down to die: and that even as hourly she dies so hourly does the child inherit life? Do they know that her body is the temple of a new soul? What men are they, in any land, who profane the sacred altars? Death was of old the just penalty of those who defiled the holy place where godhood stood revealed in stone or wood or living Bread: shall they go free who defile the temple of the human soul?

"Sure, sure," Alan breathed rather than whispered, with some such thought as this in his mind, "sure I am the priest of God, and she there my temple . . . and lo, my God!"

. . . and with that he leaned over and kissed the little rosy fingers, and the hot tears in his

eyes fell upon Sorcha's breast, so that she
stirred in her sleep, and smiled, dreaming that
a soft rain was falling upon her out of the heal-
ing Fountains of Tears that is in the midmost
Heaven.

It was at sunrise that the door opened, and
Oona entered. The child was wet with dew
which glistened all over her as though she
were a new-pluckt flower.

"Ah, birdeen, it is you!" whispered Alan
softly, lest the sleepers should wake: "See,
I have been dreaming and sleeping all night
before the peats."

Oona stared at the bed, where all she could
see was Sorcha's pale face among its mass of
dusky hair.

"Is it true, Alan? That . . . over there . . .
is *that* true?"

"It is true, dear."

"Are you *sure* that a baby has come to
Sorcha?"

"It is Himself that sent it."

"Alan, has it a soul?"

"A soul . . . Yes, sure no evil eye is upon
it, to the Stones be it said! But why do you
ask that thing?"

The child sighed, but made no answer, her
gaze wandering from Alan round the room,
and then to where Sorcha lay.

"Why do you say that, Oona? It is not a safe thing to say: sure it is not a good wishing. Who knows who may be hearing, though I wish evil to no one, banned or blest!'"

"I see no one," Oona began calmly: "I see no one, and how can *no one* hear? But I will not be for saying an unlucky thing: sure, you know that, dear Alan. *Happiness be in this house!* . . . And, now, I will be going, Alan, for I . . . "

"Going? *Hush-sh!* wait, Oona, wait: sure, you will be wanting to see the little one?"

"I want to see Nial."

"Why?"

"He must not come . . . just now."

"Why?"

"At dawn we went up to the top of the hillock, for the 'quiet people' are ever away by then, it is said. And we prayed. I prayed, and Nial said whatever I said. And then, at sunrise, we rose, and went three times round Cnoc-na-shee south-ways, and each time cried *Djayseeul!*"[1]

"And what was it you would be praying, Oona?"

[1] *Deasiul:* "the way of the south [*i.e.* of the sun] (to you!)" From *Deas*, the South, and *Seol*, way of, direction. The common Gaelic exclamation for luck, in the Highlands at any rate. Many old crofters still, on coming out of a morning, cry *Deasiul!*

"That no soul might be in the body of Sorcha's baby."

Alan stared at her, too amazed at first to be angry.

"What madness is this, lassie?"

"Sure it is no madness at all, at all, Alan! It is a good thought, and no madness. . . . For . . . for why. . . . There is poor Nial; and when Murdo met him on the hillside last night, and told him about Sorcha, Nial found me out by calling through the woods like a cuckoo, and sure a good way too, for there are no cooaks now; and then he and I hoped the baby would have no soul . . . and . . . "

"*Hush-sh! Hush-sh!* Enough! Enough! *bi sàvach!* I am not being angered with you, because of the good thought that was in your heart. But say these things no more. Come; look at Sorcha and the child."

With a light, swift step Oona moved across the room. Silently she looked into Sorcha's face; silently she stood looking awhile at the child.

Alan had no word from her, to his sorrow. Steadfastly she stared; but breathed no whisper even. Then, with a faint sigh, she turned, moved like a ray of light across the room, and, before he knew what had happened, she was gone.

Bewildered at the child going thus quietly away, he went slowly to the door; but she had already vanished. So small a lass could soon be lost in that sunlit sea of green-gold bracken.

For some days thereafter he caught at times a faint echo of her singing in the woods. Once, in a gleaming silver-dusk, he saw the imprint of her small feet, darkly distinct in the wet dew, underneath the little window behind which Sorcha lay. But she did not come again.

It was on the eve of the morning that Oona came, that Nial also, for the first and last time, beheld the little Ivor — so called after Ivor, the brother of Marsail that was Sorcha's mother, the noblest man Alan had ever known; "Ivor the good," as he was called by some, "Ivor the poet" by others.

Alan was out, talking to Anna MacAnndra, when Nial stole into the room. One hope was in his heart: that Sorcha slept.

With gleaming eyes, seeing that this was so, he drew near. The sight of the little white child, close lain against his mother's bosom, made a pain in his heart greater than ever the stillest moonlit night had done, — a suffocating pain that made him tremble.

He drew a long breath. He, too, he knew,

had once been small, perhaps white and sweet, like *that*.

Was it possible that so small, so frail a thing, could have a soul? Sure, it could not be. If not, should he not take it, and keep it by him in the forest, till the day when it could be mate to him, Nial the soulless? But if . . .

His hand touched the skin of the little rosy arm. The child opened its eyes of wonder full upon him.

They gazed unwaveringly, seeing nothing it may be: if seeing, heeding not. Had it cried, even, or turned away its head; but, no, its blue unfearing eyes were fixed upon this creature of another world.

It was enough. With a low, sobbing moan, he turned and stole unseen from the room, and so out on the hillside, and past that praying-place of Cnoc-na-shee, where so vainly he and Oona had urged that which might not be; and so to the forest, that was the home of the wild fawns, and of the red fox, and of Nial.

None, save the child Oona, ever saw again the elf-man that was called Nial the Soulless: none, though Murdo the shepherd averred that, once, as he passed through the forest in the darkness of a black dawn, he heard a wailing cry come from a great hollow oak that grew solitary among the endless avenues of the pines.

It was far within that first month of motherhood, presaged by the secret rune heard of Oona, the *Rune of the Passion of Mary*, that only women dying of birth may hear; it was within this time that an unspeakable weakness came upon Sorcha.

Day by day she grew frail and more frail. Her eyes were pools for the coming shadows of death.

Strange had been their love: strange the coming of it: stranger still was their joy in the hour of death.

For this thing upbore her, that was to go, and him, that was to stay: Joy.

Not vainly had they lived in dream. Sweet now was the waning of the dream into long sleep. Sweet is sleep that will never stir to any waking: sweeter that sleep which is but a balm of rest.

For they knew this: that they would awake in the fulness of time.

When, for the first time, the doom-word passed her lips, Alan shuddered slightly, but he did not quail.

"I am dying, dear heart!"

"Sorcha, this thing has been near to us many days. It is not for long."

"And thou wilt look to thine own dark hour with joy?"

"Even so."

"And our legacy to this our child . . . shall be . . . shall be . . ."

"It shall be Joy. He shall be, among men, Ivor the Joy-bringer."

No more was said between them, then or later.

It was in the afternoon of the day following this that Sorcha died. She was fain to breathe her last breath on the mountain-side. Tenderly, to the green hillock by the homestead, Alan had carried her. Soft was the west wind upon her wandering hands; warm the golden light out of the shining palaces of cloud whence that wind came.

He was stooping, with his arm upholding her, and whispering low, when, suddenly, she lifted the little Ivor towards him. Quietly she lay back against the slope of the green grass. She was dead.

Alan quivered. All the tears of his life rose up in a flood, and drowned his heart. He could not see the child in his arms; but he did not sway or fall. Sorcha strengthened him.

Then silently the wave of grief, of a grief that might not be spoken, ebbed. Out of the sea of bitterness his soul rose, a rock with the sun shining upon it.

Slowly he raised the child above his head, till the wind was all about it, and the flooding glory of light out of the west.

A look of serene peace came into his face: within him the breath of an immortal joy transcended the poor frailty of the stricken spirit.

When the words that were on his lips were uttered, they were proud and strong as the fires of the sun against the dawn : —

Behold, O God, this is Ivor, the son of Sorcha, that I boon unto Thee, to be, for all the days Thou shalt give him, Thy Servant of Joy among men.

There was peace that night upon Iolair. But towards dawn — the morrow of that new strange life wherein Alan and the child, with Oona mayhap, were to go forth towards those distant isles, where, as Sorcha had seen in a vision, Ivor's ministry of joy was to be — a great wind arose.

The hills heard, and the moan of them went up before it. The mountains awoke, and were filled with a sound of rejoicing.

Through the darkness that lightened momently it came down the glens and the dim braes of bracken. Many waters felt the breath of it, and leaped.

The silences of the forest were as yet unbroken. Unbroken of the wind at least: for, faint and far, there rose and fell a monotonous chanting, the chanting of a gaunt, dwarfed, misshapen figure that moved like a drifting shadow from pine-glade to pine-glade.

But as dawn broke wanly upon the tallest trees, the wings of the tempest struck one and all into a mighty roar, reverberatingly prolonged: a solemn, slow-sounding anthem, full of the awe of the Night, and of the majesty of the Day, hymning mysteries older than the first dawn, deeper than the deepest dark.

And after the passing of that great wind the forest was still. Only a whisper as of the sea breathed through its illimitable green wave.

THE END.

THE KEYNOTES SERIES.

16mo, cloth.   Each volume with a Titlepage and Cover Design.

By AUBREY BEARDSLEY.

PRICE, $1.00.

Sold by all Booksellers.   Mailed, postpaid, on receipt of price, by the Publishers,

ROBERTS BROTHERS, BOSTON, MASS.

John Lane, The Bodley Head. Vigo Street. London, W.

PRINCE ZALESKI.

BY M. P. SHIEL.

Keynotes Series. American Copyright Edition.
16mo. Cloth. Price, $1.00.

The three stories by M. P. Shiel, which have just been published in the Keynotes series, make one of the most remarkable books of the time. Prince Zaleski, who figures in each, is a striking character, most artistically and dramatically presented. "The Race of Orven," the first story, is one of great power, and it were hardly possible to tell it more skilfully. "The Stone of the Edmundsbury Monks" is in something the same vein, mysterious and gruesome. It is in "S. S.," however, that the author most fully discloses his marvellous power as a story-teller. We have read nothing like it since the tales of E. A. Poe; but it is not an imitation of Poe. We much doubt if the latter ever wrote a story so strong and thrillingly dramatic. — *Boston Advertiser.*

The first of the three tales composing this little volume is entitled "The Race of Orven," which supplies the character from whom is taken the title of the book. The other two are, "The Stone of the Edmundsbury Monks" and "The S. S." There are three maxims on the titlepage, probably one for each of the tales, — one from Isaiah, one from Cervantes, and one from Sophocles, — but they are a triple key to the spirit of book altogether. The Prince, however, rules the contents entirely, pervading them with mysticism of every imaginable character. The "S. S." tale is decidedly after the manner of Poe, full of mysterious problems in murders and suicides, to be treated with ingenious solutions. There is a morbid tendency running through the entire trinity, the author seeming to invent characters and complications only to exhibit his ingenuity in unravelling them, and in stringing on these ingenious theories the spiritual conceptions in which he is wont to indulge his thought. But the thought is both magnetic and bold, and rarely illusive. Hermitages, recluses, silences and funereal glooms, and the entire family of grotesque thoughts and things, are not merely wrought into the writer's canvas, but are his very staple, the warp and woof composing it. It is an across-the-seas collection of conceits, skilfully strung on one glittering thread by a matured thinker. The attempt is made to carve out the mystery of things from the heart of the outward existence. The men and women on whom the scalpel is made to work are real flesh-and-blood entities, of such strong points of character as to be actually necessary in developing the author's thought as much as his purpose. The book belongs to the increasing class that has come in with the introversive habit of modern thought and speculation — call it spiritual or something else. — *Boston Courier.*

Sold by all Booksellers. Mailed, postpaid, on receipt of price, by the Publishers,

ROBERTS BROTHERS, Boston, Mass.

THE WOMAN WHO DID.

' BY GRANT ALLEN.

Keynotes Series. American Copyright Edition.

16mo. Cloth. Price, $1.00.

A very remarkable story, which in a coarser hand than its refined and gifted author could never have been effectively told; for such a hand could not have sustained the purity of motive, nor have portrayed the noble, irreproachable character of Herminia Barton. — *Boston Home Journal.*

"The Woman Who Did" is a remarkable and powerful story. It increases our respect for Mr. Allen's ability, nor do we feel inclined to join in throwing stones at him as a perverter of our morals and our social institutions. However widely we may differ from Mr. Allen's views on many important questions, we are bound to recognize his sincerity, and to respect him accordingly. It is powerful and painful, but it is not convincing. Herminia Barton is a woman whose nobleness both of mind and of life we willingly concede; but as she is presented to us by Mr. Allen, there is unmistakably a flaw in her intellect. This in itself does not detract from the reality of the picture. — *The Speaker.*

In the work itself, every page, and in fact every line, contains outbursts of intellectual passion that places this author among the giants of the nineteenth century. — *American Newsman.*

Interesting, and at times intense and powerful. — *Buffalo Commercial.*

No one can doubt the sincerity of the author. — *Woman's Journal.*

The story is a strong one, very strong, and teaches a lesson that no one has a right to step aside from the moral path laid out by religion, the law, and society. — *Boston Times.*

Sold by all Booksellers. Mailed, postpaid, on receipt of price, by the Publishers,

ROBERTS BROTHERS, Boston, Mass.